Meg Perry

Promoted to Death

A Jamie Brodie Mystery

The Jamie Brodie Mysteries

Wednesday, March 8, 2017

Santa Monica, CA

Red-blue-red-blue-red-blue-red-blue...
I cracked my eyelids, barely a sliver, and squinted at the alternating pattern of lights on the ceiling of our bedroom.

Only one thing that could be.

I hadn't been sleeping well. I'd dislocated my left shoulder - *again* - three and a half weeks ago in a rugby match and was still strapped into an immobilizer. I was used to sleeping on my left side; whenever I unconsciously rolled that way, I woke up. On top of that, I had a nasty cold and was on sick leave for the week.

I didn't know what woke me this time. Whatever it was, our yellow Lab, Ammo, had heard it too - his ears were perked. As I tiptoed across the room, he rose from his own bed and followed me. Pete, my husband, didn't even twitch.

The clerestory windows in our bedroom were too high to see out of. I slipped into a pair of boxers then padded downstairs to the living room, trailed by Ammo, and peered through the blinds. The flashing lights were coming from several police cars and a fire truck, blocking 17th Street in front of me. I couldn't see anything else.

Maybe there'd been an accident at the intersection of 17th Street and Wilshire. It had been known to happen.

A couple of cops returned to their patrol cars in a leisurely fashion. I looked at the clock. Quarter past four. I doubted I'd get back to sleep, and I didn't want to risk waking Pete by climbing back into bed.

Ammo curled up on his auxiliary bed at the end of the sofa and was asleep in seconds. I arranged the pillows on the sofa and attempted to get comfortable.

Apparently, I made myself sufficiently comfy. The next thing I knew, Pete was gazing out the window, his hands on his hips. Ammo was standing beside him, his tail waving. I grunted and sat up, and Pete and Ammo both glanced around at me. Pete said, "How'd you end up down here?"

"Something woke me up. I saw flashing lights and came down to see what it was."

"There's still a patrol car out there. I'll ask 'em what happened." He rubbed one hand through his hair, making it stand on end, and took Ammo's leash from the hook by the door.

Ammo started dancing around him. "Ammo, sit."

Ammo sat, and Pete attached his leash. I poured a glass of juice and unpeeled a banana then returned to the living room to see where Pete had gone. He was on the sidewalk talking to a uniformed cop, Ammo sitting politely beside him. I ate my banana as I paced by the window, waiting for him to come back.

I was disposing of my banana peel when Pete came in. "Street racers. One ran the red light and slammed into a panel truck."

I sucked in a breath. "Dead?"

"Yeah. Driver of the truck is okay." Pete scooped Ammo's breakfast kibble into his bowl. "How are you feeling?"

"Restless. I can't sit still here. I need to go back to work." The end of spring quarter was nearing at UCLA, where I worked as a librarian. It was a busy time and my colleagues were short-handed thanks to my absence.

"Jamie." Pete crossed his arms and gave me a stern look. "Your doctor said you can go back on *Monday*. Not before."

My internist had told me to stay home while I was sick, to protect myself from further lung irritation which might trigger an asthma attack.

"It's only Wednesday."

He gave me a sympathetic smile. "Relax and appreciate the time off."

"Yeah, right. Time for a shower?"

"Yep."

In the bathroom, I carefully unfastened the Velcro straps of the restraint that was holding my left shoulder in place and kicked off my pajama pants while Pete warmed up the water. He eased me out of my t-shirt and we stepped in. He scrubbed me down first and washed my hair. Such luxury, the sensation of having someone else wash my hair. Under normal circumstances the sensuality of it would have rapidly induced a physical reaction.

But my antsy mental state didn't allow for that. The imprisonment of my shoulder, my temporary house arrest because of the cold, and the drugs I was taking for that had combined to leave me in a condition of constant distraction, bordering on crankiness.

Not an ideal mindset for romance.

Pete towel-dried my hair. He helped me into a clean t-shirt - left arm first, then head, then right arm - and secured the restraint, imprisoning my left arm. I struggled into briefs and sweatpants myself then went downstairs. I glanced out the window; the police car was gone.

Ready to leave for work - he taught psychology at Santa Monica College - Pete kissed me and ruffled Ammo's ears. "You two enjoy your day. I should be home by 2:30."

At 2:00, Pete texted. *Going to be late - kerfuffle in the department. Dinner from the falafel place?*

Sure. How late?

Should be home by 5:30. Oh, dead street racer was an SMC student.

Oh no. One of yours?

No.

Okay. Text me when you leave.

Will do.

I'd been attempting to read all day - background research for a book I intended to write on sabbatical this summer. I hadn't accomplished much, thanks to getting up every half hour or so to climb the stairs five or six times in an effort to burn off excess energy.

I *seriously* needed to get out of the house.

I gave up and texted my brother Kevin, an LAPD homicide detective. *You guys busy?*

It took a few seconds for him to respond. *Yeah. Sorry. Stabbing last night. TTYL.*

Well, crap. I looked at Ammo, sprawled in the middle of the living room floor, and had an idea. "Hey, Ammo. Want to learn a new trick?"

He scrambled to his feet, tail wagging furiously. I laughed. "Of course you do. Let me get the treats."

At 5:15, Pete texted. *Free at last. On my way to Falafel House.*

I went to the kitchen and slowly, with one hand, set the table. When Pete arrived, I called Ammo to my side, and we met him at the door. I kissed him hello. "We have a surprise for you!"

He looked skeptical. "We? You and Ammo?"

"Yup." I stepped back. "Ammo?"

Ammo gazed up at me expectantly. I said, "Play dead."

Ammo dropped to the floor, flopped onto his side, closed his eyes, and didn't move a muscle.

Pete stared for a second then burst out laughing. "I'm glad to see you've been productive."

"Ammo, up. Good boy!" I ruffled his ears and said to Pete, "It didn't take long. He's so smart."

Pete grinned. "He's not the only one."

In the kitchen, I unbagged the food while Pete opened bottles of beer for both of us. I said, "Baklava! Yum."

"I figured we both deserved it." He flopped down at the table and took a long drink.

"A kerfuffle, huh?"

"Yeah." He took a bite of dolmeh. "The agenda for tomorrow's board meeting is out. It's a special meeting to approve faculty promotions."

"And?"

"Curtis got promoted. Elaine didn't."

Curtis Glover and Elaine Pareja were two of Pete's fellow psychology instructors. I'd met Elaine at a wedding two years ago and didn't care for her. I said, "You expected that outcome, right?"

Pete said, "Yeah, but apparently Elaine didn't. I heard her yelling in Verlene's office as I was leaving. Elliott was with them." Elliott Conklin was the assistant chair of Pete's department.

I swiped a section of pita bread through hummus. "But that doesn't mean she has to resign, right? She can apply again?"

"It depends. This was a third-phase evaluation, meaning she's been rated twice by two separate panels as 'needs continued evaluation' and has been on an improvement plan for two years. Failing the review this time means the decision goes to the president and academic dean."

"The improvement plan didn't work."

"Not to the satisfaction of the panel."

I knew that promotion applications at SMC were evaluated by a panel of three other faculty members. "Were you ever on her panel?"

Pete grimaced as he sliced into a dolmeh. "No, thank God."

"Why can't she pass the evaluation?"

"There are a lot of factors that go into the decision. Retention rates, course materials, professional development activities, self-assessments, student evaluations, peer evaluations, collegiality, service to the college."

I said, "I suppose collegiality isn't her strong suit." Pete had described Elaine to me as a "suck-up" to the administration in the past.

"Right. Plus, she flunks about 40% of every class, her student evaluations are consistently terrible, and she's weak in professional development. The conferences she goes to aren't related to what she teaches, she has no desire to pursue a doctorate, and she has regular meltdowns in department meetings."

"About *what?*"

He snorted. "You name it. Last time it was because Verlene wouldn't approve a separate printer for her office."

"Why can't she use the department printer?"

"*Exactly.*" Pete picked up a slice of baklava. "She's unstable, in my opinion."

"Another example of someone who majored in psychology to figure out her own problems?"

"Elaine doesn't believe that she *has* any problems. Everyone else is the problem."

"Ugh. So - no promotion, no raise?"

"She'll receive her step raise, if they don't fire her, but she won't get the bigger bump for moving from group II to group III. If she'd get a Ph.D., she'd automatically move to group VII."

Pete had told me that at SMC, salary was determined by years of service and the classification group you were in. Group classification was based on education and experience. The higher the group number, the higher the salary. Ph.Ds. were automatically assigned to the highest group.

I said, "Without a Ph.D., can she ever reach Professor?"

"She could, but not until the end of her 20th year on faculty. And that's assuming she made Associate Professor this time. Which she hasn't."

"Sounds to me like she'd recoup the cost of a Ph.D., if it would move her to the highest group."

Pete said, "The college would *pay* for it. But she's *so* stubborn. She may have decided against it just because Verlene advised it." He sighed. "Damn. The atmosphere at the office will be tense."

"Where's her office?"

"Two down from me. Audra's between us." Audra Rock was another of Pete's colleagues. He pushed away from the table. "Let me clean up the kitchen, then I *have* to do some grading."

I made a "run along, now" motion with my free hand. "Get busy, then."

He grinned at me and carried our dinner detritus to the sink. I settled back on the sofa with my laptop, prepared for further research. Ammo looked back and forth between me and the kitchen, clearly having difficulty deciding which dad to hang out with.

I said, "Up to you, buddy."

He gazed at the stairs one last time then settled back down at my feet.

I slept more soundly that night and woke at 5:30 when Pete's alarm sounded. He slapped it off and grunted. "Why do I get up so early?"

"So you can run before breakfast. I wish I could come with you."

"I wish you could, too. I'll walk Ammo first."

"Okay, thanks." I could walk Ammo, but hanging onto him while I scooped poop was problematic with only one hand.

Pete brought Ammo back inside and kissed me. "I'm going north to Will Rogers. Be back soon."

"Okie dokie." I fed Ammo then poured myself a bowl of cereal. Since I couldn't run, swim or play rugby, I was burning far fewer calories than normal and was attempting to eat less.

I wasn't always successful.

By the time Pete got back, I'd organized my research for the day. We repeated our shower procedure and he grabbed his lunch and left for the college.

He texted me when he got to his office. *Top-secret bigwig meeting in Verlene's office.*

About Elaine?

Don't know yet.

At 2:00 he texted again. *Heading home.*

Okay. What's going on?

Tell you when I get there.

At 2:30, he arrived, wearing a grim expression. Ammo danced around him, and Pete bent down to ruffle his ears. "Hey, big guy. Want to go for a walk?"

I said, "You mean the dog, or me?"

That produced a faint grin. "Both of you."

I shoved my feet into my shoes. "Let's go. I'm desperate for some fresh air."

We walked south to avoid Wilshire and its exhaust fumes. I asked, "What was the bigwig meeting about?"

"As it turns out, not getting promoted is the least of Elaine's worries."

"How so?"

"She was sexually involved with a student. Our street racer that was killed. His name was Jason Rupp."

"Oh, dear God. He was *her* student?"

"Yes. He took social psych from her in the fall."

"And they were hooking up during that time?"

"Yeah. It started a couple of weeks into the class."

"How did the bigwigs find out?"

"A call on the anonymous tip line to the Santa Monica PD last night, telling them to check Jason's phone then contact the college. There were texts and sexts from Elaine."

"For God's sake. Hasn't she heard of Snapchat?"

"You'd think. Anyway - they were 90% sure they were going to fire her over the evaluation results. Once they'd confirmed the student affair with SMPD, that sealed the deal. Campus cops escorted her from the building."

"How old was Jason?"

"Twenty."

"Dr. Canaday must be *furious*."

Pete barked a laugh. "That doesn't begin to describe it. Verlene and Elliott both."

"Who's going to cover her classes? *Please* say it's not you."

"No. Curtis, Audra and Elliott are dividing them up."

"Can the police find out who called?"

"No. The tip line is guaranteed to be anonymous."

We turned around at South Bundy. We were a few blocks from home when Pete's phone rang. He glanced at the screen. "Unknown number."

"Don't answer it."

"I'm not." Pete pocketed his phone. A few seconds later, however, his voicemail tone sounded.

He sighed and took his phone back out. As he listened to the voicemail, his expression darkened. He deleted the message and said, "Shit."

"What?"

"Elaine wants to talk. She's parked in front of our house."

"About *what?*"

"No idea."

I had an idea - and Pete wouldn't like it. I kept my mouth shut.

When we turned the corner from Arizona to 17th Street, I saw Elaine, pacing in front of our gate. She was a petite, dark-haired woman, probably a couple of years older than Pete, in her early 40s. When I first met her, I'd observed that she possessed what my grandfather would call a "smart mouth."

Pete had told me that her classes were always the last to fill. She had a reputation for being difficult, not only academically but personally. Pete had sometimes seen students exit her office in tears.

At least once, though, one must have left with a smile on his face.

Elaine stopped when she saw us. "*Finally*. I thought you'd never get here."

Pete said calmly, "We had to walk the dog. You remember my husband, Jamie?"

Elaine favored me with no more than a sharp glance. "Can we talk inside?"

"No. We can't."

"Can we at least get off the *sidewalk?*"

Pete unlocked the gate and allowed Elaine into our front yard. He gestured to one of his brick-walled vegetable beds. "Have a seat."

Elaine looked at the ledge with distaste but perched gingerly on its edge. Pete and I sat across from her and waited. She fidgeted for a minute then said, "I need your help."

Pete said, "No."

She drew her head and shoulders back, like a cobra preparing to strike. "I haven't even told you what *kind* of help."

"I can guess. You want me to help you get your job back. The answer is no."

Clearly, Elaine had expected to be allowed to plead her argument. She was flustered. "You helped Elliott."

"No, I didn't. That was Jamie."

Elliott had briefly been a suspect in the stabbing death of his former boyfriend, several years ago. I said, "Besides, Elliott was innocent."

Elaine glared at me. Pete said, "You messed up, Elaine. I'm not going out on a limb for you. If you thought I would, you were mistaken."

Elaine jumped to her feet. "You know what? *Fuck* you, Ferguson. Fuck *you*, fuck *Verlene*, fuck *Elliott*, fuck that *asshole* Curtis Glover, fuck *all* of you. I have connections with the *Times*, and I am going to drag the fucking psychology department and this sorry college through fucking *hell*. When I'm through, no one will want to associate themselves with *any* of you." She stalked away, slamming the gate shut behind her.

I said snarkily, "That went well. Why the hell would she imagine that you'd help her?"

Pete pinched the bridge of his nose. "She thought I helped Elliott." He took his phone out. "I'd better warn Verlene."

He reached voicemail. "Hi, Verlene, it's Pete. Elaine was just here, asking for my help to get her reinstated. When I turned her down, she made threats. I figured I should let you know." He called Elliott and left the same message. "Okay. They're warned."

He locked the gate, and we went inside. He got down on the floor with the dog and was giving him an epic belly rub when his phone rang.

Pete rolled over onto his back so that he could extract his phone from his pocket, and Ammo draped himself across Pete's abdomen, clearly thinking that playtime was still in effect. I laughed. "Ammo, come."

Ammo loped over to me as Pete answered, still on the floor. "Hello? Hi, Verlene. Yes, just now. She left a few minutes ago. She said, 'Fuck you,' and included you, me, Elliott and Curtis in the sentiment. She said she had connections on the *Times* and - her exact words were, 'I'm going to drag the psychology department and this sorry college through fucking hell.' I left Elliott a message, too. Yes, Jamie's here and witnessed the whole conversation. Of course. You're welcome. Bye."

I asked, "What did she say?"

"She wasn't surprised."

"Might Elaine go to Dr. Canaday's house?" Verlene lived in the classiest section of Santa Monica, north of Montana Avenue near the border with Brentwood. Not that far away.

"She might."

On the sofa after dinner, I picked up a book, and Pete took out his phone. I said, "Who are you calling?"

"Kristen." Kristen Beach, Kevin's girlfriend and my co-worker. Pete waited for a moment then said, "Hey, yourself. Whatcha doing? No, I just have a favor to ask. Do you know anyone on the *Times?* Perfect. Could you give him a heads-up? One of our psychology faculty was terminated today, and she says she's going to the *Times* over it, that she has connections there. No, she didn't mention a name. Yeah, if he'll watch for any stories that get submitted about the college and be sure they're thoroughly fact-checked. Right. There are definitely two sides to this story. Oh - sure, we'll come up with something. Thanks, K. Bye."

I asked, "She knows someone?" Before library school, Kristen had worked in the media relations department of County-USC Hospital.

"A managing editor. She'll call him tomorrow."

"Will he handle it?"

"She said he would."

"What are we going to come up with something for?"

"A way to celebrate Kevin's birthday that he'll approve of."

"Ah." Kevin would turn 38 on March 24. He was notoriously difficult to plan celebrations for - he hated surprises and fuss. "How about a cookout at Ali and Mel's?" Alison Fortner and Melanie Hayes were childhood friends of Kevin's and mine who were now married to each other and lived in Brentwood. Their house was ideal for entertaining. "Dad and Jeff can come up. We'll have cake and presents."

"That should be acceptable. What are we going to get him?"

"When I figure it out, I'll let you know."

Pete didn't have to go to the college on Fridays this term. After breakfast, we went to our second-floor office, which also served as our guest bedroom. Pete had papers to grade, and two articles that I'd requested from Oxford through my friend Niles had arrived in my inbox overnight. Pete, as always, prepared to work by spreading books and papers all over the desk, encroaching deep into my territory. I opened the PDF articles on my tablet and began to read.

At 9:00, the doorbell rang. Pete made a sound of exasperation. I said, "I'll go."

I went downstairs, Ammo on my heels, and peered through the peephole. Verlene Canaday was outside the gate, frowning at it. I grabbed the key from its hook and let her in. "Hi, Dr. Canaday. After Elaine left yesterday, we locked the gate."

"Wise decision. Is Pete here?"

"Yes, ma'am. Ammo, fetch Pete."

Ammo bounded up the stairs. Dr. Canaday watched him in amazement. "He *does* that?"

"Yes ma'am. He's a smart one."

She smiled. "I *see* that."

Ammo trotted back downstairs, Pete behind him, and came to me as if to say, *I found him!* I rubbed his head and ears. "You are such a good boy. *Good* boy."

Pete said, "Hey, Verlene. Have a seat. What's up?"

Dr. Canaday perched on the loveseat. "When my husband went out for the newspaper this morning, he found that all of the windows on both of our cars were smashed out."

Pete groaned. "Elaine."

"Doubtless. We made a police report, but I thought you should be warned."

"I appreciate that. What did the police say?"

Dr. Canaday rubbed her chin. "They're having trouble tracking her down. She's not at home and won't answer their calls. They have a - what is it called? Some sort of notice."

Pete said, "A BOLO. Be On the Lookout."

"Yes. Making threats is one thing but taking action escalates their concern." She smiled wryly. "Mine, too."

I asked, "If she comes back here, should we call 911?"

Pete said, "I doubt that she'll come back here."

Dr. Canaday said, "She's so angry, she may not be rational. The police told us to call 911 if we saw her, so I'd assume that's their recommendation for you as well." She stood. "I should get to campus."

I said, "Thank you for stopping by."

Pete walked Dr. Canaday out. When he came back in I said, "Elaine's avoiding the cops."

"Yep. Which only pisses them off. When they do catch up to her, it won't go well."

"Wouldn't the Canadays' car alarms have alerted them?"

Pete shook his head. "They're into vintage cars. Verlene drives a VW Bug like you had, and her husband owns an old Saab. No alarms."

I said, "Elaine called Curtis Glover an asshole in her rant yesterday. Does she have something particular against him? Other than him being promoted and her not?"

"No one in the department is fond of Elaine, but I'd say Curtis likes her the least, and vice versa. Elaine imagines that Curtis gets personal favors from Verlene because they're both African-American, which is not true. She also believes that Aaron and I get personal favors from Elliott because we're all gay." Aaron Quinn was Pete's best friend at work.

"Which only leaves Audra Rock, right?"

"Right, and she doesn't like her because Audra won't join her in female martyrdom." He laughed. "Audra's got five kids. She doesn't have time to be a martyr."

I said, "From what I understand of Dr. Canaday, I can't imagine her giving *anyone* favors."

"Of course not. She'd no more do that than your Dr. Loomis would."

We'd just resumed work when Pete's phone rang. He frowned at the screen and answered. "Hey, Elliott. *What??* Well, shit. Of course it had to be her. Did you call the cops? Have you talked to Verlene? Yeah, the two police departments need to confer, if they haven't. Listen, you be *careful*. We will." He said goodbye.

I said, "Did she smash Elliott's windows too?"

"Nope. She cut down all of their shrubs."

Elliott and his partner, Stewart, lived in a rehabbed Craftsman home in Cheviot Hills. They had a lushly landscaped yard full of flowering shrubs. "Oh, *crap*. She cut them *all* down?"

"Yeah. He said it looked as if they'd had a chain saw taken to them. Although they didn't hear anything."

"*Damn*. Did you think she was capable of this level of vindictiveness?"

"I never considered it before." He sighed. "We'd better watch our backs."

We ended the day without further interruption. As Pete fixed dinner, I texted Kevin. *Cookout at Ali's for your birthday? No surprises.*

LOL, sure. I see there's a BOLO out of SMPD for a woman named Elaine Pareja. Why does that name sound familiar?

You've probably heard Pete mention her. She taught in his department until she was sacked yesterday, and she vandalized both his chair's and assistant chair's property last night. If the BOLO's still out they haven't found her yet?

Right.

After dinner, I discussed Kevin's birthday party with Ali while Pete cleaned the kitchen. When I hung up I said, "I really want to spend the evening on the deck."

He smiled at me. "Cabin fever?"

"A terminal case."

He plucked two bottles of beer from the fridge. "Come on. We'll go to the second floor. It's farther away from the pollutants."

We settled into our Adirondack chairs. I said, "Mitch hasn't sent any pictures of the house this week."

Mitch was the architect and general contractor who was building our second home in Alamogordo, New Mexico. Pete said, "No, but drywall is boring. And we'll be there in three weeks."

"True." From my phone, I retrieved the pictures Mitch sent last week of our nearly completed back patio. "How about an outdoor kitchen?"

Pete's expression was puzzled. "Why?"

"Why not? Wouldn't it be cool to have a fancy built-in grill and a sink out there? Maybe even a fridge."

"Are you serious? The indoor kitchen is ten feet away. Why do we need a second fridge outside?"

"We don't *need* it. But we can have whatever we want. Why not?"

He used his explaining-things-to-a-toddler voice, which he knew I hated. "For one thing, dearest, because we're going to generate all of our own power. Self-sufficiency, remember? A second fridge would suck up way too many watts."

In spite of his tone of voice, I had to admit… "You have a point. But what about a built-in grill? And a sink?"

"I'd rather have a mobile grill. It's more practical. And I repeat, the kitchen sink is ten feet away."

I sighed dramatically. "Okay, fine. What about a sink for potting plants and washing vegetables?"

"I don't think we need one. I'll pot plants in the greenhouse, and wash vegetables with the hose over the garden beds. Thereby watering the vegetables underneath at the same time."

"The greenhouse won't have a sink."

"No, but it'll have its own rain barrels. No sink necessary."

I gave up. "You have it all figured out."

"I hope so. I worry about whether I've forgotten something important."

"If you have, we can add on later."

"True." He gave me a sideways glance. "I'm considering writing a blog about the house and our self-sufficiency experiment."

"Yeah? As a record?"

"Yes, and a way to connect with other people doing the same thing."

"*Oh.*" I was leery of social media and its lack of privacy. "Do you have to identify us?"

"No." He picked up his phone. "I wrote this as a potential introduction. See what you think." He read, "I'm a retired cop, married to a soon-to-be-retired librarian. We're building our dream retirement home, off-grid, in the New Mexico desert. This blog will follow our progress in becoming self-sufficient."

I chuckled. "*Soon* to be retired?"

He grinned. "You'll retire eventually. Soon is a euphemism."

"You should ask Kristen which blogging platform is preferable."

"Good idea." He texted, then read her response. "WordPress, she says. And she'll help me build the blog."

"Cool." I drained my beer. "What do you have to do this weekend?"

"What do you think? Grading, grading, grading." Pete sighed. "I am sooooo sick of grading."

"Hon, you know you can quit any time you want." We were financially secure, thanks to my inheritance of $38 million from Randall Barkley, the father of the man who'd killed my mom in a drunk driving accident when I was a baby.

"Yeah, I know." Pete drummed his fingers on the arm of his chair. "That thought crosses my mind every single day."

"When are you eligible for promotion to professor?"

"At fifteen years."

"Eight more *years?*"

"Yep. I'm not going to last that long. I *may* not last until fall."

I said, "You're serious about this."

"Mm hm. I even talked to Verlene and Elliott about it."

"What did they say?"

"That I had to do what was best for me." Pete rubbed his eyes. "It's not just grading. If I teach online, I'll still have that. It's the constant politics. I realize that it exists in any sizable government organization and there's no escaping it. But I'm *sick* of it. This crap with Elaine is just one example among many. The faculty are always bitching about something, the union reps and Academic Senate are always squabbling, the board is always meddling in instruction. It's wearing on me."

I said, "I'm sure UCLA is the same. I'm not aware of it because I'm too low on the food chain." Academic librarians in the University of California system were not granted faculty status.

"See, there are advantages to not being faculty." His expression sobered. "One thing about the college - the administration will do almost anything to avoid a lawsuit. If Elaine shows up with an attorney, they'll probably pay her to disappear."

"Would she accept it? Or would she demand to be reinstated?"

"No idea."

I said, "If you resigned at the end of spring term, you wouldn't have to come back early from my sabbatical."

"I also wouldn't have to write a paper over the summer, a topic for which I still have not thought of."

"You could blog all summer. And you'd be free to stay in Alamogordo while Abby builds and installs our cabinets. That will require at least a couple of weeks."

"I'd be able to spend extra time with my dad." Jack had suffered a massive heart attack three years ago. His resulting congestive heart failure was not improving.

"Sam will be in town come September. You'd have plenty of time for her." Pete's niece Samantha was admitted to UCLA for the fall.

Pete gazed across the rooftops. "More time to cook. More time to garden. More time with Dad, Sam and you."

"Ammo would have company during the day if you were home."

He chuckled. "Are there any cons?"

"None that we can't afford."

He drained his beer. "I'll talk to Verlene again on Monday."

Before my respiratory infection materialized, we'd scheduled a group hike for Saturday morning. When I checked my lung function after breakfast, I saw that it was 85% of normal. Not sufficiently low to create abnormal shortness of breath, but definitely sub-par. I wanted to attend my rugby team's game in the afternoon, so I decided to spend the morning indoors. At 7:00, Pete buckled Ammo into his car harness and headed for Topanga Canyon to meet Kevin and Kristen; Ali and Mel; and Kevin's partner, Jon Eckhoff, and his girlfriend, my fellow librarian Liz Nguyen.

I went back to bed, intending to sleep for about another hour. I woke up at 10:00, groggy and temporarily disoriented. I sat up, scrubbing my face, and realized that the doorbell was ringing.

Ugh. I staggered down the stairs and peered out. Pete had locked the gate behind him, fortunately. Elaine Pareja was standing on the sidewalk, pressing the doorbell over and over and rattling the bars of the gate.

I wondered if the BOLO was lifted on her and decided to err on the side of caution. I went to the kitchen and called 911.

The police must have been nearby. I was still explaining who Elaine was to the dispatcher when two patrol cars rolled up. Both officers were beefy guys with nearly-shaved heads. They blocked the street with their cars. One of them apparently asked Elaine for ID, and she apparently refused to show it.

I opened the door and walked to the gate. One of the cops - according to his nametag, Officer Boone - spotted me. "Sir? Did you call in the complaint?"

"Yes, sir. This is Elaine Pareja. She's a person of interest in a property crime at the home of Dr. Verlene Canaday on Thursday night."

Elaine lunged at me. "You keep your mouth shut, faggot."

"Whoa, whoa, whoa." Boone stepped in front of Elaine. "Calm down, ma'am."

The other cop was talking on his radio, apparently confirming my information. Elaine shouted, "Keep your hands off me!"

Boone hadn't touched her. "Ma'am, I haven't laid hands on you."

I said, "No, he hasn't."

If Elaine's stare could decapitate, I'd be headless. The other cop said, "Yes, sir," into his radio, then turned to Boone. "Sarge says arrest her."

Boone said, "Ma'am, you're under arrest. Hands behind your back, please."

Elaine's arms were practically windmilling out from her sides. "I will not! You can't arrest me for ringing a doorbell!"

The other cop said, "We're arresting you for vandalism, ma'am. Put your hands behind your back, or we'll add resisting arrest to your charges."

Elaine shot me one last evil glare but allowed the cop to handcuff her and lead her to his patrol car. Boone asked me, "Who is she to you?"

I explained. He nodded as he took notes. "You say she was here Thursday evening?"

"Yes, sir. When she showed up this morning, I didn't know if the BOLO was still out, so I called just in case."

"Why would she come back here?"

"I don't know. Pete - my husband - is an ex-cop himself. She had to realize we'd call you guys."

"Is he at home?"

"No, sir. He's hiking in Topanga Canyon."

The arresting officer had locked Elaine in the back of his cruiser; he came back to the gate. "She says she's on faculty at SMC. Is that so?"

I said, "She was terminated on Thursday and escorted off campus."

The two cops exchanged some sort of signal. The one who'd stashed Elaine said, "Sarge is meeting me at the station. I'll see you later." He headed for his car.

Boone gave me a sharp nod. "Appreciate your assistance, Mr. Brodie."

"Yes, sir."

He wrapped his hand around one of the wrought iron bars and rattled the gate. "Might want to keep this locked."

"Yes, sir."

I went back inside and was surprised to see that only a half hour had passed. It felt much longer. I ate a bowl of cereal and went upstairs to struggle through showering and dressing myself.

I'd barely dressed when Pete came in the door. Ammo charged to greet me. I said, "Good hike?"

"Yep. Quiet morning?"

"Nope." I told him what had happened.

Pete was as mystified with regard to Elaine's motive as I was. "Why the hell would she come back *here?*"

"She's not thinking clearly."

"No shit. Still up for your rugby game?"

"I didn't go to the trouble of getting dressed for nothing."

"Uh huh. Let me check this." He examined my sling and tightened the straps. "That's better."

I grunted. "Okay, Dr. Ferguson. Let's go."

We reached the rugby pitch near Griffith Park about twenty minutes before the game started, where we were joined by Kevin, Kristen, Ali and Mel. I went to the bench to say hello to my mates; they all commiserated over my shoulder apparatus and restrained themselves from slapping me on the back. I wished them luck and went back to my seat, where I found Pete on the phone. "Yes, sir. No, I wasn't there. Yes, here he is." He handed me his phone. "Sergeant Ruffin, Santa Monica Police."

I said, "Hello, Sergeant."

"Mr. Brodie. Tell me about your visit from Ms. Pareja this morning."

I related everything that had happened. He said, "Neither of the officers touched her?"

"Only when she was being cuffed. Otherwise, not at all. Is she saying they did?"

"Yep." He snorted. "We've got you as a witness and body cameras that document her lying."

I said, "She threatened to sue the college last Thursday night. Maybe she's used to getting her way by threatening lawsuits."

"Doesn't seem to be working out for her."

"No, sir."

"All right. Thanks, Mr. Brodie."

"Yes, sir." I handed the phone back to Pete. "Where'd they get your phone number?"

"Probably from Verlene. Elaine's claiming police brutality?"

"Yep. They never touched her."

"Of course they didn't." Pete shook his head in disgust. "She believes cops are stupid. She's said so, many times."

"To *you?*"

"Mm hm. Miss Congeniality, our Elaine."

The rugby match was close-fought, and I was on my feet yelling frequently during the first half, which winded me. At halftime I realized the shortness of breath wasn't resolving.

Uh oh. I didn't want to alarm anyone necessarily, but... "Kev?"

"Hm?"

"I'm wheezing."

Kevin knelt in front of me. "Where's your inhaler?"

I patted my pocket. Where was it? Other side. I felt Kevin reach into my pocket. He stuffed the inhaler into my hand. I used it a couple of times, without much benefit. I stood up - we were sitting in lawn chairs - leaned over and propped my hands against my knees, bending at the waist, desperate to draw air in. Pete jumped to his feet. "Jamie? Are you okay?"

I shook my head. I was aware of someone calling 911 and someone else leading me back to my seat.

Kevin said, "Take another puff."

I did. No relief. I heard sirens and realized I was going to black out. Someone was standing in front of me. I tried to aim my upper body in that direction and let myself go.

I regained consciousness in a familiar environment. White ceiling, bright lights, yellow curtains surrounding me, background noise of beeps and voices. Someone, somewhere, was wailing. There was a dull ache in my injured left shoulder. I squinted against the glare of the lights and tried to raise my right hand. I couldn't.

Shit. I was tied down. Was I intubated? I took a breath, and the mechanical hiss behind my head answered my question.

In my peripheral vision, I could see someone's legs. Pete's. I couldn't turn my head to indicate that I was awake, so I kicked the side rail by my foot.

"Hey." Pete appeared in my field of vision. "You're back."

I tried to nod, unsuccessfully, and kicked the side rail again.

"Yeah, you're restrained. You were fighting them. You probably don't remember that."

I shook my head. That was easier.

Pete pushed the call button. "That attack was *terrifying*. I stood there like a street sign. Kevin, Ali and Mel went into action like a Nascar pit crew."

They'd had plenty of practice.

Pete said, "I'd watched you have a full-blown attack before, at Fertility Research when I was handcuffed to the post." Years ago, when we were chasing the killer of my friend Dan Christensen. "I might as well have been handcuffed this time for all the help I was."

It wasn't his fault. I kicked the side rail again. He seemed to get my drift. "But what if it had been just the two of us? We need to conduct drills so I'll be ready next time."

Drills. I rolled my eyes. He said, "I'm serious. Fire drills, earthquake drills, asthma drills."

A large bald man in scrubs came into the room; his nametag indicated that he was Vernon Washington, RN, ARNP. He said, "Look who's awake. How you feeling?"

I tugged against the wrist restraint and glared at him, which produced a wide grin. "You gonna behave?"

I kicked the rail again. Pete said, "That means yes."

"Okay." Vernon released my right arm. I wiggled my fingers and indicated that I wanted something to write with.

Vernon produced a pen and notepad. I wrote, *Tube out?*

"Maybe. I'll get the doc." He retrieved his pen and pad and left the cubicle.

I tried to sigh, which produced another prolonged hiss from the machine. I made writing motions again. Pete said, "Um -" and began searching through drawers. He produced a Sharpie and an inventory list.

I was sure I shouldn't be writing on the inventory list. I didn't care. I wrote, *How long?*

"A couple of hours."

Where?

"Glendale Memorial."

Shoulder hurts.

He grimaced. "Yeah, you kinda landed on it when you passed out."

The others?

"In the waiting room. I should probably tell them you're awake."

Yes, he should. I made shooing motions with my hand. A few minutes later, a tired-looking woman in scrubs appeared, trailed by Kevin. The woman's name tag read Erica Ramsey, MD. "Mr. Brodie. How are you?"

I gave her a thumbs up. She gave me a knowing grin. "Yeah, mister, we'll just see about that." She took her stethoscope from around her neck and warmed it up. "Deep breaths."

I breathed for her as deeply as I could, the machine assisting me. She checked my pulse and stepped back. "Let's administer another treatment with the tube in, then we'll extubate. Okay?"

I gave her another thumbs up and she smiled. "Be right back."

Kevin said, "Well, that was dramatic. You scared Kristen."

I shrugged my right shoulder to the best of my ability, and he nodded. "I know. She'd never seen anyone have an asthma attack. She was afraid you were dying."

I picked up the Sharpie and wrote, *She OK?*

"She was, once we got you here. She was embarrassed that she wasn't any help."

Pete says he wasn't.

"He actually was. A crowd gathered and he shooed them away." Kevin gave my healthy shoulder a friendly thump. "Kristen will know what to do next time."

Next time. Kevin naturally assumed there would be a next time. That hadn't always been the case.

Unfortunately, he was right.

After I was extubated, my oxygen levels dropped, as expected. I spent three more hours in the ER, getting nebulizers and IVs. By the time I was handed a fistful of prescriptions and sample meds and got the IVs out of my arm, it was nearly 7:00 pm. I was both wired - from all the drugs - and exhausted.

We entered the house through the back door, which appeared secure. Pete checked the front door to make sure there weren't any voodoo dolls stuck to the gate. There weren't.

We were both ravenous. Pete heated chicken soup and a baguette for supper and set a bowl in front of me. "There you go. Breathe in that healing steam."

"Mm hm." I tore off a hunk of baguette and began to munch. "Did you hike to Eagle Rock today?"

He frowned at me. "Shouldn't you be resting and eating?"

"I'm sitting down, aren't I? And I *am* eating. Where did you hike?"

"Temescal Ridge Trail, up to Skull Rock and back." He ate a couple of spoonfuls of soup. "I talked to the gang about leaving the college while we were hiking."

"What did they say?"

"Jon said he didn't understand why any of us were still working." Pete chuckled. "Kevin said he wondered the same thing at least once a day. He and Jon have a three-year plan."

"For what?"

"In about three years, Jon can move up to D-III. Kevin will have figured out what's next for him by then."

"Why will it take Jon that long to get to D-III?"

"Because he's only been serious about it for the past few months. He's got networking to do."

"Isn't networking just another word for sucking up?"

"Not in this case. Jon wants Homicide Special. He would only be required to suck up if he decided to aim for lieutenant."

"I wonder if Detective Simon is still at Homicide Special? He met Jon on the Stacks Strangler case."

"He is, and Jon's contacted him." Pete made a circular motion with his spoon. "The gears are moving."

"I never imagined Jon sticking with the department."

"It's growing on him." Pete grinned. "Like a fungus."

"So they all supported the idea of you quitting at the end of this year?"

"Mm hm. They came up with the same list of reasons we did." Pete trailed his spoon through his soup in a figure eight pattern. "I'm still mulling it over."

"You're going to talk to Dr. Canaday on Monday?"

"Yep."

"Maybe we should revisit our own long-term plan."

"You're right. What are you thinking?"

I held up one finger. "Sam is coming to UCLA this fall. You want to be here for at least her first two years, right?"

Pete's niece Samantha was a budding geophysicist who wanted to study earthquakes. He said, "Yes. Maybe three."

I said, "By her junior year, she'll be able to navigate on her own."

"Would Ali and Mel sort of... take Sam under their wing?"

I chuckled. "Nurture the baby lesbian? I'm sure they would. Okay, so we're here a couple of years for Sam."

"I've just gotten our garden where I want it, with the containers and raised beds. I'd hate to abandon that yet. Plus, it'll take a couple of years to fully establish the garden at the new house, and to build the greenhouse, since I can only work on that part time. When we do move, I want to already be producing food there as well."

I said, "You told me that Meredith is a gardener." Pete's ex-sister-in-law, Meredith Lagai, was going to be our full-time house sitter until we could move permanently.

"She is, and she'll help build the new garden as she's able. When will Colin start college?"

"Um - fall 2020. Three years." My older nephew, my brother Jeff's son, was completing his first year of high school. "He'll probably come to Caltech."

"Kevin and Kristen will be here for him. He won't need us."

"Right, and Ali and Mel will watch out for him, too."

Pete drummed his fingers on the table. "Sounds as if we'll be here at least two years. Three, maybe. Can you stand it that long?"

I huffed a laugh. "Oh, sure. Being away all summer is going to improve my attitude." Not to mention my lung function.

"There's another consideration. We have to decide what we'll do once we live in Alamogordo."

"*That's* a good question. I don't want to work full-time, but I want to do *something*. I suppose I could do volunteer work."

"Maybe you can volunteer at the community college library."

I frowned. "I'd prefer to be an adjunct history instructor."

"It's different, teaching at a community college."

"Of course. There aren't any graduate students."

"Mm hm." Pete sat back. "One last major consideration. How much longer can your lungs hang on in LA?"

I sighed. "Another good question. I don't know."

Sunday passed without incident. We saw nothing else of Elaine. In the morning, Pete cooked and I took a nap - the asthma drugs had kept me awake and restless most of the night. In the afternoon, he graded papers, and I searched for job opportunities for adjunct online psychology instructors that might interest Pete.

The positions were plentiful, if you didn't mind teaching at one of the for-profit online universities. I knew Pete *would* mind. I did come up with a handful of "real" jobs - one of which I was certain he would be interested in.

I copied and pasted the link into a text and sent it to him. "How'd you like to teach for Arizona State?"

His head swiveled. "You're kidding. They have a position?"

I read the ad to him. "'Seeking adjunct instructor to teach online. Intro to Psych and Abnormal Psych.' I sent you the link."

"What's the pay?"

"It sucks. Does it matter?"

He laughed. "Guess not."

A few minutes later my phone rang. Kevin. I answered, "Hey."

"Hey. How are you?"

"Much better. What do you want for your birthday?"

"Pfft. I have no idea. Surprise me."

"You hate surprises."

He laughed. "That's true. Listen, with all the excitement yesterday, I forgot to tell you about this. Your co-worker, Isabel Gutierrez?"

That took me by surprise. Isabel was our education and library science subject specialist, next in line for the directorship when Dr. Loomis retired. "What about her?"

"Her husband is an assistant DA. I've met him before, in court, but didn't *know* him. Anyway, Leo Kwasniowski is coming to trial this summer. Victor Gutierrez is on the prosecution team, and Jon and I met with him Friday morning."

Leo Kwasniowski was a Santa Monica cop who'd killed a UCLA student, Ashley Bennett, and dumped her body in the townhouse next to ours. He'd also come after me. I squawked in dismay. "Leo is still pleading *not guilty?* Even with the DNA evidence?"

DNA left in a condom at the crime scene had come back a match to Leo's. DNA from the blood and brain matter at the crime scene had matched Ashley's. The case should be a slam dunk.

Kevin said, "Yeah. He's an idiot. But I was talking to Victor about Ashley's parents, and how I'd kept in touch with them. Then it came out that I was a paralegal, and he asked me if I'd be interested in a new career."

"Doing what?"

"The DA's office has a Victim Impact Program. They have advocates on staff that guide victims and their families through the legal system. They're understaffed, and at least two-thirds of their current advocates are retiring within the next three years. They'll have a bunch of positions available, and he thinks I'd be a natural."

Kevin had always been gentle with and solicitous of the families of murder victims. I said, "I bet you would."

"I think I'd enjoy it, and there's no doubt that working with families would be more personally rewarding. Not to mention the hours will be *far* more regular."

"I'm sure the DA's office pays much less than the police department."

"Oh, yeah. I'd never have been able to do this before the inheritance."

"You don't think you'd miss investigations?"

"Not much. And I can detect vicariously through Jon. But - there's a catch."

"Uh oh. What?"

"I'll have to get a master's in social work."

"*Oh*. Uh -"

He chuckled. "That's how your name came up. I said that my girlfriend and brother were both research librarians and you all could find the most fitting program for me. He asked where you worked, voila."

"Ah. An online program, right? If they exist."

"I'd rather. That would match up with the three-year plan."

"Right. Pete told me about your three-year plan."

"Mm hm. Three years for Jon to be promoted to D-III and Homicide Special, and I could graduate by then, just in time to quit the force."

"You don't want to break in another partner, do you?"

He laughed. "No way. Kristen's out running errands today with Liz. Will you search for a program for me?"

"Okay. I'll see what's out there."

"Thanks, short stuff. See ya."

I turned my attention to locating the right social work program for Kevin. After an hour of research, I sent him a link. *Simmons College. In Boston, but program is 100% online. Field work in your own community. Best feature is the ability to build your own specialization. Most don't offer that.*

In a few minutes he responded. *Sounds fantastic. Was considering USC, but this is better. Thanks!!*

I smiled to myself. Kevin, a social worker. Who'd have thought?

Monday, March 13

It was time to return to work. I typically rode the bus to UCLA every day, but Pete drove me this morning so I wouldn't have to deal with bus fumes or other pulmonary irritants. Once inside my building - the Young Research Library - I handed my doctor's note to my supervisor, library director Madeline Loomis, and trudged upstairs, stopping first at Liz's office.

Liz was on the phone; she pointed to the chair across from her desk. I deposited my lunch into her mini-fridge and sat down. She was saying, "I realize that, Greg, but I cannot meet with you at 2:00 every day. My reference shift is 1:00 to 3:00, and I can't switch that. No, I *cannot* change it today. No, I eat lunch at noon. Noon to three is entirely off limits. I can meet with you at three every day *this* week, but I can't guarantee that will work next week. Once classes start, I'm going to have a slew of research workshops to lead, and those are at random times. I can't promise you one time for the whole term."

I raised my eyebrows; she rolled her eyes. "Why don't we do this? You call me every Monday morning, like you just did, and we'll schedule our times for the week to come. Yes. This week, 3:00 every day. No, we can't schedule next week. No, it will *never* be 2:00."

I snickered and she stuck her tongue out at me. "No, I can't schedule the research workshops around you. The needs of the many outweigh the needs of the one, Greg. Always remember that. I'll see you at three. Bye." She hung up and groaned.

I said, "A special snowflake?"

"The worst example of helicopter parenting I've ever seen. He's 26 and has been a full-time student since he was three. He still lives at home, and his mom came with him to his first meeting with me." Liz waved her hand in disgust. "Anyway. How are you?"

"Meh. Stodgy from lack of exercise and irritable from asthma meds."

"I bet. We missed you Saturday on the hike, but having an asthma attack out in Topanga Canyon would *suck*. How's your shoulder?"

"Pain free, as long as it's immobile. What's going on around here?"

"Not a thing. Is Pete going to resign today?"

"I don't know. He's going to talk to his chair. Pretty sure he's leaning that way."

"He sounded like it on Saturday. What does Kevin want for his birthday?"

"No idea."

"You're no help."

"Get Jon to ask him." I stood up. "I have to play catch up this morning. See ya."

Mid-morning, I got a text from Pete. *Appointment with Verlene at 4:00. Might be late picking you up.*

OK. Plenty to do here. Good luck.

He sent back a smiley face.

We didn't have much business at the reference desk, as most students had completed their research for the quarter and were now writing and revising. At 1:30, our patron and friend, former monk Clinton Kenneally, appeared on schedule, his expression solemn. "The word of the day is *vilipend.*" He bowed and walked away.

Liz found the definition. "'To hold or treat as of little worth or account; to express a low opinion of.' Huh. That's not related to anything happening here." Clinton's words of the day were often spookily pertinent to some situation in which either Liz or I found ourselves.

I said, "I hope it's not related to Santa Monica College."

My hope was in vain. At 5:15, Pete texted me. *Leaving campus now.*

A half hour later, he pulled up in the drop-off circle and I climbed in. "Hey, how'd it go?"

"I resigned, effective at the end of spring term. June 10."

"Dr. Canaday wasn't surprised, was she?"

"Not by that, no. She may resign herself."

"*Why?*"

"Elaine got reinstated."

"*What??* How the hell did *that* happen?"

"I'm not sure. It was over Verlene's protestations."

"Let's just throw the faculty promotion process out the window, shall we? Not to mention sleeping with a student! How the fuck are you all supposed to work with her now?"

Pete set his jaw. "I'm *not* going to any longer than I have to. Verlene and Elliott may both resign in protest."

"Holy *shit*. How to decimate an entire department in one move."

"Yeah. Everyone else will be job hunting, too."

"Can Aaron afford to take the time to find a desirable job?"

Aaron's husband, Paul Thayer, was one of the top home stagers in Los Angeles. "Yes, Paul's income is far higher than his. Verlene and Elliott can both be choosy, too. Curtis and Audra can't quit without having somewhere else to go."

"Was there *any* reason given?"

"Elaine was terminated because of her involvement with our student, on top of her poor evaluation. None of that has changed. I don't understand what has."

"Maybe she knows something damaging about someone influential."

"It would have to be someone *incredibly* influential. For the college to potentially expose itself to a lawsuit from the union and the state faculty association... I can't imagine what could have overridden that."

"Would your college president do it?"

"No. He wouldn't. And the board of trustees has never interfered in *that* way, to my knowledge. They vote on faculty hires, but it's supposed to be a formality. They've never stated a position on a faculty firing. Besides - a majority of the board would have to vote to reinstate her. I can't see that happening."

When we got to the Y, we found side-by-side treadmills and stepped on. I couldn't run without uncomfortably jarring my shoulder, but I set a steady uphill walking pace that wouldn't overtax my lungs. Pete built up his pace until he was running hard, slightly uphill, legs pounding, jaw grimly set. When he was about to drop with exhaustion, I said, "You should start cooling down."

I could tell that he thought about objecting, but then he tapped the controls and began slowing down. I slowed my own pace until we were both walking comfortably. Finally, he sighed deeply and stopped. "Shower at home?"

"Yeah."

In the parking lot, Pete turned his phone back on; his voice message alert chirped immediately. He checked the screen. "Elliott, Aaron and Curtis."

"All wanting to discuss the events of the day."

"No doubt."

Pete began returning calls as soon as we got home. Elliott, only four years from retirement, was still on the fence about his decision. Aaron, after discussions with both Dr. Canaday and Paul, would hand in his resignation tomorrow, effective at the end of spring semester.

Pete called Curtis as he opened a pill bottle for me. "Hey, man, sorry it took a while to get back to you. What's up?" He listened for a full minute. "No, I'm gonna teach online. Adjunct. Jamie found several positions. No, at real schools. Yeah, he can add me to his insurance. *How* much? Good God. No, of *course* not. You have to take care of your family. Yes, and I'm sure Aaron would, too. You bet. I'll see you tomorrow." He ended the call and sighed.

I said, "Curtis can't resign."

"Not yet. His wife works, too, but for a small dental practice. He has the kids on his insurance. If she adds the three kids and Curtis to hers, it'll cost $2250 a month."

"Holy *crap*. He's going to search for another job, right?"

"Yeah. He was afraid that we'd think he wasn't supporting us if he didn't resign right now."

"And you'll write him letters of recommendation."

"Sure. We all will. Audra, too, if she decides to move."

"It's gotta bite, leaving a tenured position."

Pete shook his head. "I can afford to be an adjunct. Curtis and Audra can't."

After Pete walked Ammo, we showered, and Pete strapped me into my spare shoulder apparatus. I threw our sweaty clothing and my sweaty restraint into the washing machine, then checked UCLA's academic calendar. "My spring quarter ends June 16. We can take a few days to get squared away, then head for Oxford."

"We'll have to visit Alamogordo before we fly out, to close on the house and get Meredith settled."

"Yeah. We should probably buy our plane tickets."

"Sure."

I bought tickets for June 26 - August 26, flying in and out of San Diego, since my dad was dog-sitting for the summer. "Suppose you'll be teaching by the end of my sabbatical?"

"It depends. Possibly that very last week."

"We won't be any place without internet. You can do all your prep while we're gone."

"That's assuming I *get* a job somewhere."

"You'll get one."

"I wish I was that confident."

I set aside my laptop. "So what's the worst that could happen? You're unemployed for a while. It's not like you don't have plenty to do."

"True. Speaking of which - when we get back from the UK, we should spend the rest of your sabbatical time in New Mexico. We can build the greenhouse then, and Abby can do her installation." Kevin's ex-girlfriend, Abby Glenn, was a carpenter who also built furniture and cabinets.

"Good idea. I'll work it out with her."

Tuesday, March 14

As Pete drove me to work on Tuesday, I sent Abby a text. *Hey, Abs. Remember, a few months ago I mentioned doing built-ins for us at the new house? It's time to schedule that. Call me when you get a break.*

I had back to back student appointments from 9:00 until 12:00, all with students writing dissertations on recent American history topics. Ugh. I hadn't seen an ancient history-related dissertation for a couple of years. They were outstanding students, though. At least I didn't have the issue that Liz did with her overly parented student.

At lunch, Kristen said, "I have the official word. Kevin wants no gifts. He said a cookout would be enough."

I sighed. "In that case, he gets whatever I decide he should have."

Kristen grinned. "Exactly. Did Pete resign yesterday?"

"He did, and he wasn't alone." I told Liz and Kristen what had happened.

Kristen said, "My editor friend at the *Times* called me this morning. He got a pitch from one of his reporters about 'dark doings' in the SMC psychology department and turned her down."

I said, "So Elaine followed through on one of her threats. She must have threatened someone else to get reinstated."

Liz asked, "Will you ever find out what happened?"

"I don't know. If Elliott has the scoop, he'll probably tell us after neither he nor Pete is working there anymore."

Abby called while Liz and I were at reference. We weren't busy, so I left Liz with her permission and went into Café 451 to answer. "Hey, Abs."

"Hey, you. How *are* you?"

"I'm fine." No need for details. "How's business?"

"It's booming. I quit Eddie's crew about six months ago, right after I last talked to you, and I'm working ten hours a day on my own. I have a website now, and the jobs are pouring in."

"No kidding! That's fantastic. Are you still living with Amy?"

Amy was Abby's sister, divorced with three young children. "Yeah, there are too many benefits for both of us to stop doing that. Anyway - your house is nearly complete?"

"It will be by summer. We're going to be away for a while in June and July, but how would the end of August or beginning of September work for you to spend a couple of weeks in Alamogordo? You could stay at the house."

"This far ahead, that's fine. I thought you meant like next month."

"No, no. They're still installing drywall now. I can send you electronic copies of the blueprints with indications of what we're considering. And we want you to charge us whatever you would normally. It's not like we can't afford it."

She laughed sharply. "I guess not. Okay, it's a deal. Do you want something similar to what we did in your home office?"

"Yes, at least in the new office and library. We can get together and talk about it when you have a free evening."

"Super. Send me the blueprints, and I'll study them."

"I will. Thanks, Abs."

"Thank *you*. Tell Pete hello."

"I will."

When I got back to the desk, I texted Pete. *Abby's on board for August-September installation. What's going on?*

Elaine's back in her office - smug until she found out nearly everyone was planning to leave. Audra and Curtis are applying to Phoenix, Capella, etc. and several positions with Los Angeles Community College district.

What about Dr. Canaday?

She's been in admin offices most of the day. Not back yet.

I told him what Kristen had said about her editor pal at the *Times*. He responded, *At least nothing will come of that. See you this evening.*

I sighed. Liz asked, "Bad news?"

"No, just continuing mess at SMC. There is some good news." I told her about Abby.

"Oh, I'm glad to hear that." She grinned. "I can't *wait* to see your new house."

"You can use it for vacations, if the New Mexico desert is a place you've always dreamed of going."

"Jon would *love* Roswell."

I snickered. "He'd fit right in."

When Pete and I got home, the house smelled wonderful. I said, "Roast chicken?"

"And mashed potatoes. I felt like comfort food."

I sat at the kitchen table, watching Pete mix the milk, potatoes and butter. "Anything else happen today?"

"Dr. Canaday got no satisfaction from the administration. Elaine stays."

"They'll have to scramble to staff the teaching schedule for summer."

"That's a bright spot in all this. The academic dean is no fan of Elaine's. She'll be teaching overloads all summer. The dean says it's because they *can't* hire adjuncts that quickly. It's more likely that they *won't*."

"So whoever it is that Elaine has dirt on, it's not the academic dean."

"No. Maybe it's someone on the board, not in the administration. The president and dean have always supported the faculty's right to manage the promotion process ourselves. They've never reversed a decision like this in the past."

"But you said the board hadn't, either."

Pete sighed. "Maybe it's someone at the state level. What would you think about replacing this screen door with a wrought iron gate?"

Our back door was protected by a screen door - which didn't provide much protection. "That's a good idea. Do you believe Elaine is still a threat?"

"She did contact the *Times,* and probably vandalized Verlene's cars and Elliott's landscaping. I don't want to take any chances."

"What's happening with the vandalism charges?"

"I don't know."

"Helen has a door like that."

"Yeah. After dinner, I'll ask her who installed it."

I decided to brave the outdoors for a walk after dinner, with a fortifying puff from my rescue inhaler. We stopped by our neighbor's house first. Helen Quintero, a retired school administrator, lived in the townhouse at the opposite end of our building. She was in her garden and gave Pete the name of the metalworking company that had installed her back door. We chatted with her for a minute, then followed our route up Arizona and back, talking about the New Mexico house as we strolled.

It was nearly 7:30 and starting to get dark when we neared home. We were laughing about something as we turned the corner onto 17th Street - and our laughter died immediately as we saw Elaine Pareja pacing in front of our gate.

Pete muttered, "Oh, for God's sake."

I hissed, "What does she *want?*"

We stopped in front of the gate. Pete said, "Elaine. What the hell are you doing here?"

"First, I want to apologize to Jamie. For what I said the other day." She seemed to be supremely uncomfortable. "That was uncalled for, and I'm sorry."

In my experience, people said what they *really* thought in times of stress, but I didn't argue with her. "Thank you."

"Second -" She stopped and waved her hands in the air. "You can't all *quit.*"

Pete said, "Sure we can."

"But -"

Pete held up his hand. "Elaine. Did you seriously believe that any of us would sit meekly by and be bullied by you and whoever engineered your reinstatement? You said you wanted to drag the department through the mud. You've gotten your wish; you've wrecked the department. The only person to blame for your predicament is yourself."

"But I have to teach *five classes* in *both* summer terms."

"Tough shit."

"You're all *tenured.* You'll have to start all over again."

Pete said, "I'm going to teach online as an adjunct. The others are *willing* to start over. None of us want to work for an organization that can be blackmailed into subverting the promotion process and retaining a sub-competent and unethical faculty member."

Elaine was getting mad again. "Are you accusing me of *blackmail?*"

"I'm saying that there's no logical reason for the college to reinstate you. The only conclusion I can draw is that you're holding something over someone in a high position. If that's how the college wants to operate, that's on them, but the rest of us have professional reputations to consider. We won't change our minds." Pete's gaze dropped to Elaine's waist. "Elaine. Are you wearing a *gun?*"

What the *fuck?* I froze, fearing that any movement on my part might produce a disastrous result. Elaine scowled. "So what? I have a permit."

Pete's tone was far more casual than mine would have been. "I'm feeling threatened by that, Elaine."

"*You're* feeling threatened?" She barked a laugh. "Too damn bad, pal. I've been put through *hell* because of the rest of you. I *intend* to be threatening. *All* of you are going to be very, *very* sorry."

Pete raised an eyebrow. "It is not in your best interests to threaten us."

"Pah!" She whirled away and stomped down the sidewalk.

We watched until she turned the corner onto 17th Street. I let out the breath I'd been holding. "Holy *shit*. Should we call the police?"

"Yes." Pete reached into his pocket for his phone. "I'll call that sergeant I talked to on Saturday."

I unlocked the gate as Pete made the call, then locked it behind us and hurried into the house. Pete spoke with the police for a few minutes. When he hung up I said, "How did you spot the gun?"

"She kept waving her hands, which lifted the edge of her jacket. As cops, we were trained to scan people we encountered for guns. I guess my training kicked in."

"You were so *calm*."

He grinned at me. "So were you."

"Ha! Only outwardly. I was afraid that any movement would provoke her."

"Same here. When someone's aggressively disturbed, it's best to handle them calmly."

"Could you tell what kind of gun it was?"

"Looked like a .38 Special."

I inhaled deeply and blew out another breath. "You're calling those gate people tomorrow, right?"

"First thing in the morning."

Wednesday, March 15

I'd been at work about an hour when I got a text from Kevin. *Just submitted application to Simmons. They have staggered admissions. Might be able to start in May.*

Cool! Did you talk to anyone there?

Yeah, grad student adviser. She was very encouraging.

You'll have papers to write.

Lucky for me I have two personal librarians, eh? :-)

About an hour later, I got a text from Pete. *Back door gate to be installed tomorrow afternoon.*

Yes! What's going on at SMC?

Curtis found his tires slashed this morning, and Elaine called in sick.

She wasn't sick last night. She's plotting something else. Watch your six.

Roger that.

Thursday, March 16

By the next morning, I felt healthy enough to tackle riding the bus. On the way to campus, I downloaded an app to my phone that allowed me to count down to a particular date. I entered June 10 - Pete's last day at SMC.

I couldn't wait until he was free, although I wasn't sure he felt the same way.

I should probably ask him about that.

When I got to my office, Kristen was leaning in Liz's doorway. She said, "Has Elias contacted you yet?"

Elias Pinter was one of the West LA Division homicide detectives, along with Kevin, Jon, and Jill Branigan. "Elias? No, why would he?"

"Hm. No reason."

I shook my finger at her. "Oh, no. You don't get to pull that. What's…"

Kristen said, "Ah, here they are now."

I turned to see Elias and Jill approaching. Elias said, "Jamie, good morning. Hope we're not interrupting anything."

"Not at all. I just got here." I unlocked my office door. "Come in. What's up?"

Elias lowered his bulk into one of my chairs. "Elaine Pareja was found dead in her home this morning."

I froze, my finger on the power button on my computer. "You're… *Dead?*"

"Yep. Deceased, expired, shuffled off this mortal coil."

Elias had a reputation as a joker. Jill rolled her eyes. She asked, "When was the last time you saw her?"

"Tuesday night. I've seen her several times over the past week." I told them everything.

Jill took notes. Elias listened, his eyes narrowed. "She was that poisonous that no one wanted to work with her?"

"It wasn't that. They've been working with her for years. The issue was that she wasn't performing up to standards *and* she was fooling around with one of her students *and* the college overruled the department, the chair, and the academic dean and reinstated her. No one wants to teach in a system that would completely overrule the faculty promotion process. Plus, it's psychology, where professional behavior is held to high standards. Being involved with a student is equivalent to being involved with a client. It's ethically disastrous. If she had a license, she would have lost it."

Jill said, "Repeat the conversation that you and Pete had with her on Tuesday night."

I repeated it. Elias said, "She threatened everyone in the department?"

"Yes."

"That was Tuesday, and she called in sick on Wednesday?"

"That's what Pete said."

Jill asked, "Would you describe her as distraught?"

"I'd describe her as *furious*." There was something in Jill's tone... "Wait a minute. Did she commit *suicide?*"

Jill didn't answer my question. "Would that surprise you?"

"It would *shock* me. That doesn't fit my impression of her at *all*."

Elias asked, "With Elaine gone, will everyone change their minds about leaving?"

"Pete won't. Her death won't erase what the college was willing to do."

Jill said, "You and Pete were home last night?"

"Yes, ma'am. We got home from the Y about 7:15 and didn't go out after that. Do you want to check the records of our alarm system? I have the app right here." I waved my phone at Jill. "I can show you."

Jill smiled. "Sure, let me see."

I opened the app for our home monitoring system and showed Jill the details of our entry last night, complete with video. "And here's the next time either door opened, when we walked the dog this morning."

"That's slick." Jill recorded the information.

"All right." Elias slapped his knees and stood. "Thanks, Jamie."

"You're welcome. Is this your case?"

"No, it's Kevin and Jon's. They're at SMC. We're the B team on this one."

"Where did Elaine live?"

"The Palisades."

I said, "How the heck does a community college assistant professor afford the Palisades?"

Jill raised an eyebrow. "Good question."

Elias and Jill left. Kristen had disappeared, probably to her office. Liz said goodbye to the detectives and came into my office. "Kevin and Jon got called out at 4:15 this morning."

"Ugh. Who found her?"

"I don't know. Is Pete in trouble?"

"No. I showed Jill last night's records from our alarm system. She hinted that it might have been suicide."

Liz shook her head. "Poor SMC. They've been through it the past few years, haven't they?"

"Yeah, but so have we. That's life in the big city."

She laughed. "See you at lunch."

I texted Pete, realizing that I wouldn't hear from him for a while. *Elias and Jill just left, told me what happened. Call when you can.*

Then I got to work.

I didn't hear from Pete until 3:15, back in my office after our reference shift. When I answered the phone, he said, "Hey, I'm at home. The gate installers are here - although now it feels like locking the barn door behind the horse."

"The gate is still a good safety feature. Kevin and Jon spent the day at the college?"

"A chunk of it. They brought campus cops with them and kept us isolated from each other. We could teach our classes but couldn't talk to anyone else."

"Had the students heard?"

"No, and we didn't tell them. Elaine hasn't been identified in the media yet."

"How could she afford to live in the Palisades?"

He snorted. "Excellent question."

"Jill asked me if I'd be surprised if Elaine committed suicide. I said yes, but... was she shot to death?"

"I don't know. She had that gun with her the other night, though... maybe?"

"So you haven't had a chance to talk to anyone else in the department?"

"No."

"I wonder if anyone will change their minds about the resignations?"

"I'm sure Curtis and Audra will."

Hm. I said, "Are they in trouble?"

"I don't know. Kev and Jon were in their offices a long time."

"They're the only ones that really needed to hang onto their jobs."

"Mm hm."

"Who found Elaine?"

"The newspaper carrier. She noticed that the front door was wide open and there were lights on in the house. It didn't look right to her, so she parked and went to the door. Elaine's body was within view at the far end of the entry hall."

"If Elaine killed herself, why would the door be open?"

"It wouldn't. But then why would a murderer leave the door open?"

"I don't know." I heard banging and the sound of a drill in the background. "How's the installation coming?"

"Almost done. It's a simple job, since the door is a standard size."

"Where's Ammo?"

"I wrapped his leash around the sofa leg. I'm with him."

"Okay. I'll see you in a couple of hours."

"Will you stop for Indian food? I got less work done in the office than I hoped. I'd rather not cook tonight."

"Sure. See ya."

When I got home, I climbed the steps to the back deck to check out our new door. Ammo was on the other side, lying on the kitchen floor. He scrambled to his feet and began his "You're home, you're home, you're home" happy dance. I peered through the screen and called, "Yoo-hoo, I'm home."

Pete trotted down the steps from the second floor. "Wonderful. I'm starving." He unlocked the door and let me in, then locked it again. "How do you like the door?"

"It's perfect. Did they give us extra keys?"

"One for each of us, a spare for Kevin, and one for the hook."
He hung the key on the hook beside the door. "Yours is upstairs on
the desk."

I dropped the food onto the table. "Let me wash my hands, and
I'll be right back."

Pete had divided the food when I returned, and we dug in. I said,
"How long do all of you in the department have to abstain from
talking to each other?"

"We don't, now that we've left for the day. I spent about an
hour on the phone with Aaron after I talked to you."

"What did he say?"

"Elaine showed up at his house late Tuesday evening, after she
left here. He had a similar confrontation to the one we had with her,
ending with her threatening the entire department. He had to call the
Pasadena cops to convince her to go away."

"He didn't let her in the house, did he?"

"No, he made her stand on the front porch. He said she was
yelling. His neighbors heard it."

"Did he see her gun?"

"No. I suppose she might have left it in the car."

"Is he going to reconsider leaving?"

"No. He has a friend at USC with whom he's written several
articles who's been bugging Aaron to join his lab for years." Aaron's
specialty was physiological psychology, the most biologically based
in the field. "He'll start July 1."

"Will he be faculty?"

"No, he'll be the research lab coordinator. The pay is less, but
he'll still be able to do research and publish papers, which is what he
wants." Pete tore a section of naan and scooped up a bite of food.
"Elaine was busy on Tuesday night. She must have slashed Curtis's
tires, too."

I said, "Whoever was behind Elaine's reinstatement will be
outed now. They'll have to tell Kevin and Jon how that happened."

Pete's smile was laced with satisfaction. "And *why* it
happened."

Friday evening, when I got home, Kevin and Jon were on the living room sofa. I kicked off my shoes at the door. "Is this an official police visit?"

Jon said, "Yep."

"You don't require my input, do you?"

Kevin said, "Nope."

Pete said, "Sorry about Date Night."

We hadn't planned anything. Maybe he was subtly informing Jon and Kevin that they were interrupting. I said, "We'll catch up tomorrow."

I helped myself to a beer. Kevin was asking, "So who's still leaving the department?"

"Aaron and me. Elliott, Audra and Curtis will all stay, at least for now."

"What about Dr. Canaday?"

"She hasn't indicated one way or the other what her thoughts are."

Jon said, "You're not only leaving because of Elaine's reinstatement."

"That's just the last straw in a very thick bundle. It's like you said last weekend. Most days I don't know why any of us are still working."

I sat on the bottom step between the living room and kitchen and rubbed Ammo's belly. Kevin said, "Tell us about Curtis."

Pete nodded, as if he'd been expecting the question. "He was just promoted to full professor, been at the college fifteen years. His students adore him - his intro classes fill first. He's been a super colleague, always willing to cover classes. He's respected at the college and is continually being asked to serve on committees because he's such a productive and dependable worker. The only person that had any issue with him was Elaine."

"You said before you thought that Elaine's attitude toward Curtis was racially motivated."

"Yes."

"What about away from SMC?"

"He was in the Army before he went to college. I don't know anything about his service record except that he saw combat in Desert Storm. He's married with three kids, all middle school - high school age. His wife works as the insurance billing person in a dental practice."

Kevin said, "Ex-military, huh?"

Jon said, "He knows how to handle guns."

Pete raised an eyebrow. "So she *was* shot."

Kevin said, "At close range, with her own gun, which was lying beside her right hand. Neither of her hands tested positive for GSR, though."

"So it wasn't suicide?"

Kevin shook his head. "We doubt it."

Jon asked, "What's Curtis's area of psychology?"

"The psychology of communication. He also teaches our research methods class. And intro to psych, of course."

Kevin said, "You don't believe he's responsible for Elaine's death?"

"No. Does he not have an alibi?"

Jon said, "No. He doesn't."

Pete asked, "Where does Curtis say that he was?"

Jon said, "The old standard. Out driving around. He'd been arguing with his wife about whether he should ditch the college or not. She wanted him to resign - she said they had adequate savings to see them through a few months. He said that was their kids' college fund, and he wouldn't consider risking it. He and his wife both say that he left the house at about midnight and didn't come home until five in the morning."

Elaine's body was discovered at 4:30. The timing fit. Pete's expression was grim. "Did Audra have an alibi?"

"A shaky one. Her husband's out of town, and she said she was home all night. But her kids are teenagers. It's possible that she could have slipped out for a couple of hours. They're able to be on their own for a while."

"Did Elaine visit her on Tuesday?"

Kevin said, "Audra says no. She lives in the Valley. Elaine might not have had time."

Pete said, "Elaine may have thought she could talk to Audra on Wednesday."

Jon said darkly, "Maybe she *did* talk to Audra on Wednesday. *Late* Wednesday. Right before Audra shot her."

Kevin asked, "Do you know anything about Audra's history with guns?"

Pete said, "I don't know that she *has* a history with guns. But we've never discussed it."

I raised my hand. Kevin grinned. "Yes?"

"Have you figured out how Elaine could afford a house in the Palisades?"

"Not yet. We won't get her financial records until Monday."

Pete said, "With no GSR on her hands? That sounds like a killer who *doesn't* know much about guns."

I thought, *Good news for Curtis? Bad news for Audra?*

Jon checked his watch. "We should scram. We have an appointment to talk to Jason Rupp's parents."

The dead street racer. Kevin said, "Thanks, guys. Sorry about date night."

Pete said, only half-jokingly, "Don't make a habit of it."

They left, Kevin shooting me a grin on the way out. I said, "Trying to make them feel guilty?"

"Yes. They have dozens of other people they could be talking to."

"But they like us the best. I take it they don't have any suspects other than Curtis and Audra yet?"

"Not yet. Forensics has a shitload of prints and trace to process from Elaine's house." Pete rubbed his eyes. "How was your day?"

"Uneventful. How was yours?"

"I got a ton of work done. Do you want to go out to eat?"

"No. Let's have popcorn or something."

"Mm. Popcorn and beer." He stood and edged past me on the stairs.

"Do you really believe Curtis or Audra couldn't have done it?"

Pete gave me a shrewd look. "I didn't say they *couldn't* have. I just don't think they *did*."

Saturday, March 18

On Saturday morning, we went to the farmers' market and were walking home, laden with vegetables, when Pete's phone rang. He checked the screen. "It's Elliott."

We went inside; I began unloading eggplants and zucchinis from Pete's backpack as he answered the phone. "Hi, Elliott. No, just got back from the farmer's market. What's up? Oh. Um - let me check." He lowered the phone. "Dinner invitation for this evening from Elliott at his house."

I said, "Why not?" We had no other plans.

Pete said into the phone, "We'll be there. What time? Okay. Want me to bring anything? All right. See you then." He hung up. "Aaron and Paul are invited, too. Seven o'clock."

"What's on his mind?"

"He didn't say." Pete joined me in the kitchen and began sorting vegetables. "Want roasted veggie subs for lunch?"

"Sure."

We'd no sooner cleaned up from lunch than Jon and Kevin arrived. I opened the door and called to Pete in the kitchen. "Quick, hide the dope! It's the heat!"

Jon laughed; Kevin just shook his head. "I assume we're interrupting *something*."

"If you can sit and talk in the kitchen, you won't interrupt Pete's cooking."

Pete was making pasta sauce, chopping herbs and peeling the plum tomatoes we'd bought at the market. He said, "I assume you're here on official business?"

"Yep." Jon had a briefcase, from which he removed a laptop computer with an LAPD property tag. "We want you to watch this surveillance video."

Pete asked, "Of what?"

Kevin said, "Of Elaine going into a hotel in Anaheim a week ago Wednesday. We want to see if you recognize anyone else."

I said, "How'd you come across that?"

"The credit card slip from the hotel was in her purse."

"That's not very secure, is it? Carrying video around on a laptop?"

Jon said, "The link is password-protected on an LAPD server. It requires several layers of authentication to get to it. We use the same system for body camera footage."

He booted the computer and moved through multiple screens, typing passwords as he went. Pete asked, "Did you learn anything from Jason Rupp's parents?"

"No." Kevin shook his head sadly. "They had no idea he was involved with an instructor. They knew he was seeing someone, but he'd told them it wasn't serious. They did turn over one of his textbooks and his toothbrush in case we need to exclude his fingerprints or DNA."

I asked, "Were there prints on Elaine's gun?"

"Only her own."

"But you said there was no GSR on her hands."

"There wasn't. The killer had to have worn gloves, so he or she didn't wipe the gun."

Jon turned the monitor toward Pete. "Here you go. See if you recognize anyone."

Pete set aside his knife and sat at the table. "This is the entry to the hotel?"

"Yes. For several hours before and after Elaine came in. We deleted the sections where no one was coming or going." Jon tapped the trackpad to run the video.

I watched over Pete's shoulder, mostly out of curiosity. Pete watched, chin resting on his palm, shaking his head *no* each time a new face appeared. Elaine came in and stopped at the reservation desk, paid with a credit card and was handed a key, then moved out of the picture.

Pete said, "She checked in under her name?"

Kevin said, "Yeah. Probably so the person she was meeting wouldn't have to."

I said, "Are you sure she met someone? Maybe she had some reason for going there herself."

Kevin said, "She met someone. Coming up -" He pointed at the screen. "Now."

A man wearing an overcoat, suit and a hat pulled low on his forehead, carrying a briefcase, his face turned away from the camera, came through the door and crossed the lobby. Kevin said, "He didn't check in. Went straight to the elevators. The footage from the hallway outside her door shows him entering her room and leaving two hours later, but his face is still obscured."

Pete said, "His gait isn't familiar."

I asked, "What businessman wears a hat anymore?"

Jon said, "Only one who attempts to sneak into hotels anonymously."

Pete watched the rest of the video, shaking his head each time someone else moved through the door. When it ended, he said, "I didn't see anyone that I recognized."

Jon sighed. "Neither has anyone else."

I asked, "Could the hotel meeting be unrelated to the college?"

"At this point, anything's possible." Jon shutdown the laptop and stowed it.

Pete said, "There's no *way* this was unrelated to the college."

Kevin shrugged. "You wouldn't think. But maybe Elaine was involved in something outside the college. Her financial records might be revealing when we get them on Monday."

Pete said, "Just so you know, Elliott's invited us to dinner this evening, along with Aaron and Paul. He didn't say why."

Kevin lifted an eyebrow. "Have you talked to him since Elaine's murder?"

"No. You kept us apart Thursday, and I didn't go to the college on Friday."

Jon said, "If he has anything intriguing to say, you know who to call."

Kevin added, "And don't say anything yourself."

Pete spread his hands. "Like what? I don't *know* anything."

Jon said, "Unfortunately, neither do we."

Once Kevin and Jon had departed, Pete went back to his pasta sauce. I watched him for a minute, then asked, "Pete?"

"Hm?"

"Is Elaine's death bothering you?"

His hands stilled on the cutting board and he turned to me, his expression curious. "Why?"

"I'm just wondering. You haven't said much about it, other than discussing details of the investigation. I mean, you worked with her for seven years. You must have emotions about it."

He resumed chopping. "Now that you ask... I should probably feel worse than I do. It's a tragedy for her family. But she was *such* a lousy coworker. She made our lives hell in so many ways over the years. It's hard for me to dredge up any sadness over her."

"Do you feel bad about not feeling bad?"

"Not particularly. That's the cop in me, I think. Every murder victim was somebody's child, but if the victim was a shitty human being - you feel for the family, but that's one less shitty human being on the planet." He glanced at me. "Are you disappointed in me?"

"Why would I be? I lived with Kevin for six years. He was the same." I smiled. "Sometimes I forget that you were a cop."

He snorted softly. "I *never* forget."

Elliott moved to his Cheviot Hills Craftsman after selling his industrial Venice loft, where he'd lived with Matt Bendel. Matt had been killed in a case of mistaken identity in the Venice house, three and a half years ago.

I'd met Elliott's husband, Stewart Moss, at Aaron and Paul's wedding a little over two years ago. Stewart had also accompanied Elliott to Pete's and my wedding six months after Aaron's. He was an ophthalmologist and seemed like a congenial guy, but I hadn't had the opportunity to talk with him much. He and Elliott had only been married a few months - one of the several couples that we knew who'd panicked after the presidential election and had hastily wedded before January 20.

When we climbed onto the front porch, I heard barking. Elliott opened the door, accompanied by a pair of black and white Cardigan Welsh corgis dancing around his feet. "Thanks for coming."

Pete bent down to pat the dogs. "Of course. Who are these guys?"

"Bonsai and Sushi. They were originally Stewart's dogs."

Bonsai and Sushi sniffed us suspiciously, then decided that our Labrador-scented pants and shoes didn't pose a threat and trotted away. It appeared that Stewart was the cook in the family; he stepped out of the kitchen wearing a barbecue-style apron and waved, then disappeared. Whatever he was making - something Italian, I thought - smelled wonderful.

Aaron and Paul had already arrived. Elliott led us back to the den, where we found them with glasses of wine. Paul greeted me with European-style air kisses. "Can you *believe* what's happened?"

"No. Pete said that Elaine came to visit you guys too."

"She most assuredly did. *I* kept out of her way, but I could still hear every word she screeched." Paul shuddered. "So could our neighbors. I've gotten an earful about *that*, let me tell you."

Elliott handed me a glass of wine and asked, "How's your shoulder?"

"Coming along, thanks."

Paul fingered the strap of my shoulder restraint. "You're such a *brute*."

Uh huh. Paul was chronically flirtatious. "You've always said we were butch."

There was a pass through between the den and the kitchen; Stewart stuck his head through it and said, "You can come to the table now."

When we were seated Elliott said, "Verlene's having dinner with Curtis and Audra this evening. We decided to - not divide and conquer, because we're not conquering anything, but for ease of entertaining."

Aaron said, "You're not going to ask us to stick with SMC, are you?"

"No." Elliott smiled, but it didn't reach the solemn expression in his eyes. "I've always expected that you'd both eventually step down for wider opportunities. It's a shame that it's happening all at once, but I don't blame you. No, Verlene and I just want to strategize about the rest of the semester."

Pete said, "Elaine's classes are covered."

"Yes, and Verlene and I will teach the bulk of the summer classes ourselves. We'll both be working all summer anyway, interviewing candidates for your positions." He smiled again. "That's why we make the big bucks."

Pete said, "Curtis and Audra will be available to teach."

Elliott's expression shifted slightly. "We hope so."

We were all silent for a moment, considering the possibility of Audra's or Curtis's guilt - then Aaron asked what I'd been wondering. "Do you know how Elaine got reinstated?"

Elliott frowned at his glass of wine. "All I know is that the board met to vote on the promotions on Thursday, the day she was dismissed. Then they held an emergency meeting the next afternoon. Verlene called me late last Sunday night; the academic dean had called her, after hearing from the president. Elaine was being reinstated. No reason provided to Verlene, or the academic dean. If the president knows, he's not telling."

I said, "So it was the board, not the administration."

"Apparently. Not that the outcome is any different." Elliott attended to his eggplant parmesan - which was beyond delicious.

Pete asked, "Are you staying?"

"Yes. At least until Verlene and I can get the department back on solid footing, which will take as long as I have left before I can retire from instruction. Then I'd like to join the counseling services of a college or university. Be a real psychologist. Have the opportunity to make a difference in students' lives, rather than just teaching them."

Pete had a thoughtful expression on his face. I made a mental note to ask him about that later, wondering if a counseling job might appeal to him.

The rest of the evening proceeded more jovially. We got into a discussion about rehabbing Craftsman houses - Elliott, Aaron and Paul, and my dad had all done so, and Paul had seen a lot of examples in his work. Then Paul began telling hilarious stories about some of the houses he'd staged. By the end of the evening we were all totally relaxed.

As we left, thanking Stewart for the wonderful meal, Elliott shook our hands. "Thank you again for coming, and for all your outstanding work over the years. I'm sorry things have ended this way, but I know you guys will be happier in your new positions."

Aaron said, "We'll get through spring semester, the police will catch Elaine's killer, and this will all fade to a distant memory."

When we got to the driveway and our cars Aaron asked Pete, his voice low, "Did you recognize the guy in the hat on that surveillance video?"

"Nope. You?"

"No. It's frustrating. I feel like we should know who killed her."

Pete said, "How could we? It's turning out that we didn't know anything about her."

"True." Aaron gave us a half-smile. "See you Monday."

As Pete was backing out of the driveway I said, "Should I text Kevin? Tell him Elliott doesn't know anything?"

"Sure."

I typed, *Elliott strongly suspects that Elaine's reinstatement came from the board. They had an emergency meeting day after she was canned. He doesn't know anything else. He's staying at the college.*

He responded immediately. *OK, thanks.*

I set my phone in the cup holder and said to Pete, "You had a thoughtful look on your face when Elliott said he wanted to be a college counselor."

"Did I?"

"Mm hm. Did that sound appealing?"

"Yes. I'm not sure why I hadn't considered it before." Pete drummed his fingers on the steering wheel. "I went into psychology because I wanted to make a difference for young people. At the time I didn't intend to do that via teaching."

"It's worked out that way, though."

"Yeah, so far - but I've been teaching in person. I doubt that I'll be able to cultivate the same relationships with online students. But - " He sighed. "A counseling position would be nine to five. We'd be tied down again."

"As long as I'm still at the library, we're tied down anyway."

He gave my left leg a friendly smack. "Points to ponder."

Sunday, March 19

Pete and I were in the garden - I was pulling weeds one-handed - when I got a text from Kevin. *Do some research for me?*

Sure.

Two things. First, SMC Board of Trustees members, procedures, minutes, anything you can find that might be pertinent. I know it's all online but I don't have time.

OK, want me to email results?

Please. Need to find out how Elaine got reinstated. I suspect the answer lies with the board.

Will do. What's the other?

Whatever you can find on a company called Ethicgreen. We found a contract that Elaine had signed with them a few years ago, and some products of that brand around her house.

Products?

Soap and other cleaning stuff.

OK. Won't be able to get details until I can go to Rosenfeld tomorrow. The Rosenfeld Library served UCLA's Anderson School of Management. Many of their resources could only be accessed by students, staff and faculty of the business school.

That's fine. We're spending today reading all of Elaine's email anyway.

I sent a gagging emoji. He responded, *No shit. Thanks.*

I went inside and returned with my laptop. Pete glanced at me. "Quitting?"

"Kevin asked for some research. Do you know anything about your Board of Trustees?"

"Nope. Couldn't even tell you most of their names."

I Googled *Santa Monica College Board of Trustees.* Their page on the SMC website popped up immediately. I first searched for the minutes and found a long list going back to 1998.

I found that the meeting held on March 9, the day Elaine got fired, was a special meeting. The routine board meetings were on the first Tuesday of each month. The minutes for the special meeting weren't available yet, but the agenda showed that it was held to approve the faculty promotions.

I checked and found that in previous years, the faculty promotions had been approved during monthly meetings.

I said, "Pete? Why did the board call a special meeting to vote on the promotions? It's always been done in a routine meeting before."

"Ah - I heard about that. The promotion list wasn't complete in time for the regular March meeting, and HR had to have the finalized list by March 15."

"I can't find where that ever happened before."

"Huh." Pete thought about it. "I can't see what that would have to do with Elaine's death. The promotion list is provided to the board by the academic dean."

"Okay." I turned back to the board information. The meeting the day after the special meeting was listed as Emergency Meeting/Closed Session. The minutes weren't posted for that one, either, but the agenda was.

It wasn't long. The first page was comprised of a description of the rules governing the calling of an emergency meeting. The second page was a list of the board members.

The statement after that said, "Closed Session - pursuant to Code 54957: Consideration of the appointment, employment or dismissal of an employee."

Bingo. I created an email to Kevin, and copied and pasted the agenda into it.

I scanned through the list of minutes to see when the last emergency board meeting had been held, and found that it was June 7, 2013. The day of the shootings at SMC.

The day I'd rushed home to ensure that Pete was all right, only to find him being kissed by his ex, Luke Brenner, on our sofa.

I shook my head to get *that* image out of my mind and read the minutes of that emergency meeting.

There were no details. So it wasn't likely that the minutes for the emergency meeting on "appointment, employment or dismissal of an employee" would have details either.

So much for transparent governance.

I dug into the Board of Trustees' policy manual to ferret out anything that Kevin might find useful. There were a few lines about the board's ability to terminate contract employees - i.e., faculty - but none about their ability to reinstate them. I copied that, and the sections on when, how and why special and emergency meetings could be called into Kevin's email, then added a statement of my own.

Board comprised of seven members. All have to be residents of Santa Monica or Malibu. They're elected positions. Only a quorum - four - necessary to hold a meeting. Bottom line - emergency closed meetings don't have to provide details. You will be able to find out which board members were at the meeting. I'll check back for minutes.

The agenda for the board meeting contained the names of the board members. I Googled them to find out who they were, and added the information to the email message.

Board members:

1. Augusta Skipper, chair. Wife of land developer - Bob Skipper, Hardhat Holdings, Inc. Lives in Malibu.

2. Harold Hendricks, immediate past president, Santa Monica Hotel-Motel Association. Owns hotels. Lives in Santa Monica.

3. Celine Bachmann, retired from administration at Pepperdine. Lives in Malibu.

4. William Ostrander, judge, LA Superior Court. Lives in Santa Monica.

5. Charles Mullins, retired USAF brigadier general. Lives in Santa Monica.

6. Zane Wong,

I stopped cold when I saw Zane Wong's information.

6. Zane Wong, CFO OF ETHICGREEN, INC. Holy SHIT. Coincidence?? Lives in Malibu.

7. Sierra Barrientos, lawyer in real estate firm, Dawson, Duncan and Hill. Lives in Santa Monica.

I sent the email and pulled up UCLA Library's newspaper database. There was very little about Ethicgreen. I sent a couple of brief articles to Kevin. He replied, *Thanks. HUGE coincidence with Ethicgreen and Zane Wong.*

Right? I'll get financials for you tomorrow.

I closed my laptop and set it aside. Pete glanced up. "Find anything?"

"Maybe." I told him about Zane Wong and Ethicgreen. "Ever hear of it? Or him?"

Pete shook his head slowly. "No. *Cleaning* products?"

"That's what Kev said. Is that strange?"

"Not necessarily, but I'd have bet money that Elaine had a housekeeper."

"Maybe she did, and the housekeeper used those products. So... if Elaine was involved somehow with Zane Wong, I can see him wanting to get her reinstated, but why would he want her dead?"

Pete lifted an eyebrow. "Depends on *how* they were involved."

Monday, March 20

I walked into the library on Monday morning to find a commotion at the circulation desk. It seemed to be a cheerful commotion, but I couldn't see what was going on. Dolores Lopes, one of our other librarians, was standing at the back of the pack. I leaned down and said, "What's going on?"

She jumped a little, and turned. "Oh, Jamie, you startled me."

"Sorry. What's up?"

She beamed. "Andy and Jessie just got engaged."

"No kidding!" Andy Narahashi, a circulation specialist, and Jessie Gaither, an interlibrary loan specialist, had been dating for nearly three years. "Why can't I see them?"

"They're sitting down. I mean, they *just* got engaged. Andy proposed at the circulation desk, because it's where they met."

"*Oh.*" I stood on my toes to see over the heads in front of me, and got a glimpse of Jessie's dark head and Andy's darker one, surrounded by the circulation and ILL staff. "I'll go upstairs and come back when the crowd has thinned."

"Okay. I'm going in." Dolores began weaving her way through the clumped bodies.

I stopped in the librarian office suite, where Liz was standing in Kristen's doorway. Liz said, "Hey, you heard the news?"

"Yeah. I couldn't get close to them to say congratulations, though." I elbowed her and nodded toward Kristen. "Seems like three years is the popular tipping point, eh?"

Liz and Jon had gotten engaged after three years of dating; Pete and I had gotten married at that point. Kristen shook her head, grinning - she and Kevin were coming up on two years this summer. "Guess you'll have to wait and see about that."

I shook my head in amusement. "I'm going upstairs. You coming?"

"Sure, sure. Back to work." Liz waved at Kristen. "See you at lunch."

We climbed the stairs to the second floor. Liz flopped into one of my chairs as I booted up my computer. "Jon and Kevin spent fourteen *hours* reading that dead woman's work email yesterday."

"Did they find anything?"

"They have a new list of people to talk to, but nothing promising. They're getting the subpoena for her personal email and phone records today."

Mid-morning, I went downstairs, stopping at circulation first to congratulate Andy, then moving on to the office that Jessie shared with Erin Parks, the other ILL tech. Erin was out; Jessie was frowning at her monitor. I said, "Congratulations, you."

She brightened. "Oh, thank you! It was a total surprise. I had no idea he was going to propose."

"Do you have a date?"

"No, but it'll probably be late summer. When do you get back from sabbatical?"

"I'll be back in the country by August 26."

She grinned. "Sometime after August 26, then."

On the way back upstairs my phone dinged with a text - an invitation from Ali and Mel to Kevin's birthday party on Saturday afternoon. His actual birthday was Friday. I RSVP'd, then considered what I might get for him and, coming up blank, texted my dad. *Ideas for a gift for Kevin?*

None. Was going to ask you the same.

Ha! I'll probably end up getting him a book.

Me too. See you Saturday.

You're all coming?

Yep. Jeff's not on call. My brother Jeff was a veterinarian. *Let me know if you have any gift brainstorms.*

I will.

Hm. Kevin enjoyed reading, but he had very little time to devote to it. His personal library was scanty. I knew he had full sets of Robert Crais's Elvis Cole series, Jonathan Kellerman's Alex Delaware mysteries, and Michael Connelly's Harry Bosch novels, but I was almost positive he'd never read Ross MacDonald.

Time to change that. I visited the website for my favorite mystery bookstore in Pasadena and placed an order, then sent Pete a text - *Just ordered Kevin's birthday gift.*

Then I sent an IM to Sheila Meadows at Rosenfeld, UCLA's business library. *You free?*

I am. Have a question?

Yes. Can I come over?

Sure. Visit your great-granddad at the same time.
Ha! Be right there.
What's the company? I'll get started.
It's called Ethicgreen.
OK.

When I appeared at Sheila's door, she glanced up from her monitor and smiled. "Come on in."

I stopped at the large framed photo on the wall of a grimy group of West Virginia coal miners. Both Sheila's grandfather and my great-grandfather, Emory Jarrell, were pictured. I said to my great-grandfather's image, "Hey, Emory."

"He's doing well."

"I see that." I crossed the room to stand behind her desk. "Find anything?"

"Yeah. Ethicgreen is a multi-level marketing company of sustainably sourced household products, headquartered in Malibu. Privately held, incorporated in California, in existence since 1997. What are you searching for?"

"Anything you can find. It's for a police investigation."

"Another murder?"

"Yeah, a faculty member at Santa Monica College."

"Oh, I heard about that on the news." Sheila grimaced. "You want me to email this to you?"

"Could you send it to my brother? Kevin dot Brodie at lapd dot org."

"Sure." She began downloading and attaching documents. "How's business at YRL?"

"Steady. What's new here?"

"Two items, one of which I hope will lead to the other. I'm graduating with my Ed.D. at the end of spring quarter, and our director is retiring as of June 30."

"Cool! And you're applying for the position?"

"Yep. I don't know that I'll get it, with limited experience as a library administrator, but we'll see."

"You have plenty of other administrative experience."

Sheila had spent ten years as a manager with the Florida Wildlife Commission before going to library school. "True. I'm hoping that will count."

"That's great! Congratulations on the degree."

"Thank you." Sheila worked her keyboard and mouse for another minute. "Okay, he's got all their financials, annual reports and incorporation details. Do you want me to search for news items?"

"No, I did that yesterday. Thanks, Sheila."

"You're welcome."

I said goodbye to Emory and went back to my office. As I entered the building I got a text from Kevin. *Got the stuff. Tim will go through the business information. Thanks.*

Tim Garcia was Kevin's supervisor and had an MBA. *You're welcome.*

When Clinton appeared at the reference desk, I was searching our databases for anything else I could find about Ethicgreen. He stopped and smiled. Liz said, "Hi, Clinton."

"Good afternoon. The word of the day is *bryology*." He bowed and walked away.

I found the definition. "The branch of botany that deals with mosses, liverworts, and hornworts."

Liz said, "Hey, a word that doesn't have particular application to us. That hasn't happened for a while."

"No - unless some of these Ethicgreen products are made with mosses."

She leaned over to see my screen. "Who are they and why are you researching them?"

I explained. "Kevin and Jon are searching for connections between Elaine Pareja and the SMC board. This is the first one that's turned up."

"Is that significant?"

"They don't know yet, but it's a remarkable coincidence."

"What are you looking for?"

"*Anything.* I haven't found much."

"If the company hasn't done anything newsworthy, that's good, right?"

"Either that, or they're experts at hiding stuff."

She grinned at me. "You're getting cynical in your old age."

"I've always been cynical. I just used to disguise it better."

That made her laugh.

When I got home I greeted Ammo and kissed Pete. "Did you get my text?"

"Yeah, it was funny, I was talking to Kevin when it came through."

"Oh, they came back to campus?"

"Yeah, they'd sealed Elaine's office on Friday but hadn't had the opportunity to search it yet. They were there most of the day. Elias and Jill came with them, and searched everyone else's offices."

"Did they find anything?"

"No. But they received Elaine's bank records. They left about the same time I did to start going through those. What did you get Kevin?"

"The collected works of Ross MacDonald."

"Excellent choice. Want to set the table?"

"Sure." I began taking plates from the cabinet. "What was the atmosphere at work today?"

"Extremely quiet. People whispering even when there's no need. Having the police there inhibits free expression. Even our classes were docile."

"It won't last. After the Stacks Strangler murders, things were getting back to normal at UCLA after a couple of weeks."

"I guess so. Did you find out about that company?"

"Yeah. It's a multilevel marketing company of green household products. Maybe Elaine was one of their salespeople."

"She never tried to sell me anything."

"If SMC is like UCLA, she wouldn't be allowed to. No soliciting at work."

We sat down to eat, and my phone buzzed with a text from Kevin. *Bank records show Elaine was getting monthly payments from Ethicgreen. Major $$.*

Pete says he never tried to sell her anything.

No one else in the department mentioned it when we interviewed them. Have to go back and ask if anyone knew about it.

I showed Pete the messages. He said, "So *that's* how she could afford the Palisades."

"And a housekeeper."

Pete pointed his fork at me. "And *maybe* that's how she kept a young boyfriend."

Tuesday, March 21

Mid-morning, I was in my office when Kristen appeared at my door. "Liz, Erin and I are throwing an engagement party for Jessie and Andy weekend after next, at my house. Only their *friends* are invited."

I grinned. "Got it. Should we buy a gift?"

"They both love board games, and the only one they own is Scrabble. We thought it would be fun to give them a bunch of games then play one or two while we're there. I'll draw up a list."

"Cool! Sign me up for Clue."

She laughed. "The party isn't a surprise, but the games are. So keep that aspect of it quiet."

The library grapevine was in high gear, however, and word got out. Liz and I had just returned to our offices from the reference desk that afternoon when Stephen Atcheson stormed down the hall toward us.

Stephen was a librarian who'd been teaching English as an adjunct, and was dumped on us after being accused of making inappropriate advances to several female students in his classes. He was a thin-skinned, slovenly boor who'd unsuccessfully hit on every unmarried female librarian in the building - including Jessie. None of us could stand him.

His words were polite, but his expression was furious. "May I ask you something?"

Liz and I stopped. I said, "What?"

"In your office?"

I sighed and unlocked my door. "Aren't you supposed to be on the circulation desk?"

"I'm on break." Stephen glared at Liz, who'd followed us inside. "My question is for Jamie."

I said, "Liz is always welcome in my office. I'm not so sure about you."

He gritted his teeth. "Why wasn't I invited to Andy and Jessie's party?"

Liz and I both stared, open-mouthed. I said, "Why the hell *would* you be?"

"Nearly everyone was."

I tried to be patient. "Are you friends with Andy or Jessie?"

He squirmed. "Not especially."

Liz said, "The party is for their *friends*."

"They're friends with everyone else in the library?"

I said, "Not *everyone* else is invited."

"Everyone else in access services is invited."

Liz and I simultaneously shook our heads. Liz said, "Where the *hell* did you *ever* get the idea that people socialize with others who aren't their friends?"

I said, "Just because you work together doesn't mean you spend time together *away* from work. I have to work with Gerry O'Brien, but you'll never see him at one of my parties."

"But you're playing board games. *I* like board games too."

Liz burst out laughing. I said, "Oh, for God's sake. What are you, five? I bet you like lasagna too, but that doesn't mean I'm inviting you to dinner tonight."

The expression on Stephen's face was a mix of anger and bewilderment. Liz managed to get herself under control. "Listen, Stephen, there are books you can read about socially appropriate behavior. You should consult one. Or ten."

I said, "Stephen, if you say *anything* that alerts Andy or Jessie to the fact that we're playing board games at their party, we will make you very sorry. And I bet your break is over."

He turned and stomped toward the elevator. Liz and I watched him go. Liz said, "Can you *believe* that asshole?"

"No. He's - unique."

"Pfft. That's one word for it." Liz unlocked her own door. "Our break's over too."

When I got home I greeted Ammo, sniffing the air. We weren't having lasagna, it seemed - I didn't smell anything cooking. "Hey, I'm home."

Pete called to me from the kitchen. "Dinner's almost ready."

I went to the kitchen and kissed him hello. "I don't smell anything."

"That's because we're having cold food. I made dolmeh and Greek salad."

"Yum! Let me wash my hands."

When I came back to the kitchen Pete was tossing a huge bowl of salad. "Grab a plate and claim your dolmeh."

When we were both seated I took a bite of the dolmeh. "Oh, wow. That's maybe even tastier than the Falafel House's."

He was pleased. "I found the recipe online."

I downed one and cut into another. "What's going on at work?"

"Not much. Everyone else in the department got phone calls from Jon, asking about Ethicgreen. Elliott said that Alice Greeves sold it too."

"Ah." Alice Greeves taught statistics at SMC and often collaborated with Elliott on scholarly papers. "Was she in Elaine's downline?"

"Elliott didn't know. He and Stewart went to a meeting at Alice's house once about the stuff, but Elaine wasn't there."

"Have Kevin and Jon talked to Zane Wong yet?"

Pete shook his head. "Don't think so."

"Why not?"

"I expect they want to establish some facts about Ethicgreen independently before they tackle him. See if his story is consistent."

I poked at my last dolmeh. "I still don't see what his motive would be. If Elaine was making a lot of money for the company, which she was, seems like he'd want her to continue that. I can see him being responsible for instigating her reinstatement, but why would he kill her?"

Pete shook his head. "No idea."

Wednesday, March 22

On Wednesday when I got to work I had an inbox full of email from history and philosophy instructors, asking to schedule their spring quarter research instruction sessions. I sighed, gazing at the screen in despair. The least favorite element of my job was speaking to freshman-level "introduction to fill in the blank" classes - but, even though I worked at the graduate library, I was the history and philosophy librarian. The classes were my responsibility.

I took them in the order they'd arrived and began scheduling.

Liz came in as I was working through my list. "Whatcha doing?"

I told her. "I hate undergraduates."

She laughed. "No, you don't. Undergraduates become graduate students. Some of the students in those classes will grow up to be history majors. Pretend you're only talking to them."

"That won't work in philosophy classes."

"Then pretend they're all going to study Plato and Socrates. At least that's within your favorite era."

"You like teaching, don't you?"

"Yeah. But then, all aspects of political science and public policy fascinate me. You're a sub-sub-specialist so you're a subject snob."

"I know. I'm terrible."

"Nah. You're just getting burned out in a profession that was your second choice. To quote my husband, 'I don't know why any of you are still working.'"

When Clinton approached the reference desk, his expression was grave. "The word of the day is *predacious*." He bowed and walked away.

I said, "That has to be related to predators."

Liz found the definition. "Yep. Predatory; given to victimizing or destroying for one's own gain." She frowned. "What does that have to do with?"

"I don't know." But I wondered if it was related to Santa Monica College.

I got home to find a large box, flaps folded back, sitting on the ottoman in the living room. The house smelled like vegetable soup. Pete glanced around the kitchen cabinets. "Hey."

"Hey." I kicked off my shoes and scratched Ammo's ears. "What's the box for?"

"Donation. I cleaned out the top level kitchen cabinets. There are gadgets in there that I've never used. I figure if I haven't by now, I never will."

I picked up an object I couldn't identify - a metal circle with handles extending from either side. "What the hell is this? It looks like a dangerous sex toy."

Pete grinned. "That's a thing to cut the corn off a cob."

I dropped it back into the box. "What's wrong with a paring knife?"

"Exactly. That's why it's in the box."

When we were seated and eating Pete asked, "How was your day?"

"Slow. It's exam week. How was yours?"

"I had lunch with Kevin."

"Ah. What was he doing on campus?"

"Interviewing Alice Greeves. She *was* in Elaine's downline. Elaine recruited her."

"Does Alice know Zane Wong?"

Pete shook his head. "She met him once at a meeting, that's all. Kev said she was able to explain how the company operates."

"Does she earn much money from it?"

"No. You know how multi-level marketing works. Only the people at the top can make a living from it."

I slurped a spoonful of soup. "How was Elaine so successful? She wasn't that close to the top, was she?"

"No. Most of her business was online. Kev and Jon found her sales website. Said it was professionally done, and she had a blog, Facebook page, Twitter feed, the whole works, dedicated to selling Ethicgreen. She had customers worldwide. Jon was at the station reading all of that while Kevin spoke with Alice."

I raised an eyebrow. "And yet Elaine was able to teach full-time *and* fool around with a student. Busy lady."

"Busier than we knew, apparently. Alice told Kev there are rumors of other students."

"Whoa. Did she name names?"

"No. She wasn't close enough to Elaine to have that information, but she told Kevin who might be. Do you know a librarian of ours named Annie Snow?"

"No. Has she been there long?"

"Only about four years. I barely know her myself, but somehow she and Elaine were friendly. Kevin talked to Annie after lunch. She *did* know of another student, and also said that Elaine had a steady boyfriend of appropriate age before she got involved with these students."

"Ooooh. Did Annie name names?"

"Only the student. Since he's still alive and FERPA is in effect, the school won't release any information to Kevin. Annie didn't know the earlier boyfriend's name."

"How is Kevin going to find the student?"

Pete shrugged. "He has the name. He'll just have to ask around until someone tells him something."

"Did you know Elaine had a boyfriend?"

"Nope. And Kev and Jon didn't find anything in Elaine's email that hinted at anyone who might be a boyfriend."

"Have they gone through her phone contacts?"

"Yeah, and they've spoken with them all. No exes in the bunch."

I sighed. "God, this is time-consuming. I hope Kevin gets to come to his own birthday party."

I'd barely gotten to work the next morning when I got a text from Pete. *Skype interview with Arizona State tomorrow morning.*

I sent back, *Woo-hoo! That was fast.*

Yeah. Hope it's a positive sign.

I spent most of the day tweaking and checking for broken links in research guides, something I did before every new quarter began. It was tedious work. When I got home I was thirsty for a beer. Pete had made spinach and eggplant lasagna - probably not Stephen's favorite - which I inhaled along with my beer.

Pete chuckled as I chowed. "Slow down. You're eating too fast to savor my creation."

"Sorry." I set my fork on the plate. "Anything new on Elaine's case today?"

"Yeah. I had lunch with Kev and Jon again. They'd been to Malibu to talk to Zane Wong."

"Oh. What did they find out?"

"Not much. He claimed that he didn't know Elaine well. He did tell them what went on in the emergency board meeting where Elaine was reinstated."

"Was he the one who instigated that?"

"No. He said he voted against it. Five of the seven board members were present, and the other four voted for Elaine."

"Did he provide the names?"

"Yep. Skipper, Hendricks, Barrientos and Ostrander. He also gave them the names of everyone in Elaine's downline and upline."

I asked, "Did they find out about Elaine's other student?"

"Yes. Turns out Aaron had him for general psych last fall. The kid's name is Taylor Vinson. He was in Elaine's social psych class this semester."

"Was Taylor a competent student?"

"No. Aaron said he was lazy and didn't read instructions. He was on the water polo team, so he thought the rules didn't apply to him. He got a C minus in Aaron's class. Yet, *somehow*, he had an A so far from Elaine."

I laughed. "It's a miracle."

Aaron had graciously stopped at the Pasadena mystery bookstore to pick up Kevin's gift, and brought it to work for Pete. After dinner I tried one-handed to wrap the two-volume set, and failed. Pete was grading in the office. I carried the books and my supplies to the desk and set them down. "Help."

He grinned and deftly accomplished the task. "How much longer are you in the restraint?"

"Another week, as of Saturday. Then six weeks of physical therapy before I can do anything."

"You'll be able to run."

"Yeah, but not swim." I tested my shoulder against the straps of the sling, which didn't budge. "I'm over this."

"I know." He smiled sympathetically. "At least you're not left-handed."

I'd settled down to read on the office sofa when I got a text from Kevin. *Can you ask Sheila, tomorrow, to help with research again?*

Sure, what company?

Bluefire Inc. The college is considering the purchase of property along 16th St. west of campus, across from stadium. Bluefire owns most of it.

Isn't that a residential area?

Yeah. Bluefire's been buying up houses as they go on the market for past two years and turning them into rentals.

Who told you this?

College president. Went back to talk to him again this afternoon. He told us the college wanted the property, but he didn't know who owned it. We checked property records. Also - oh, hell. Gonna call you right now.

I laughed as my phone rang and answered, "Thumbs getting tired?"

"Yes. Anyway, the president said the college wants to build a new student services complex along 16th Street. Does Pete know anything about that?"

"Let me ask." I lowered the phone and said, "Pete. Know anything about the college building a student services complex along 16th Street?"

"Um - yeah. Grant Schaeffer mentioned it a couple of weeks ago. They're getting a new library out of it."

"Ah." I brought the phone back to my ear. "Did you hear that?"

Kevin said, "Yeah. The president said it was in the preliminary stages. They haven't bought the property yet."

"Okay, I'll ask Sheila to find out about Bluefire. What did he tell you about Elaine's reinstatement?"

"That it was against his recommendation. But he serves at the pleasure of the board of trustees, so he's not in a position to push back."

"Thanks. Can you ask Pete something else?"

"I'll put you on speaker. You can ask him yourself." I sat beside Pete at the desk and set the phone between us.

Pete said, "Ask me what?"

"About Elaine's academic publishing record. When we searched her house and office, we found no copies of the articles she'd written. That's odd, right? I know Jamie has his."

Pete frowned. "Yeah, I have mine too. Most of us file a few copies in case another researcher requests one, although that's much rarer these days thanks to databases."

"That's what I thought. We got her personnel files today and they list her publications, but we didn't find any."

I said, "She sold ethically sourced household products. She may not have wanted to have a lot of paper lying around."

Pete said, "That's possible. For all her faults, Elaine was an enthusiastic environmentalist."

"Yeah, maybe." Kevin sounded skeptical. "Jamie, can you dig up her publications for me tomorrow?"

"Sure. Do you have a list of them?"

"Um - I can write one. Can't you just search for her name?"

"Yeah, but I might miss something."

Kevin sighed. "Okay. I'll ask Elias to send you a list tomorrow."

"Thanks. I'll go ahead and start the search without it. You're gonna have to start paying me for all this research, you know."

"You're such a comedian. See you tomorrow."

On the bus the next morning I texted Kevin. *Happy Birthday!*
He sent back a smiley face. Probably all he had time for.

When I got to work and had dealt with my email, I sent an IM to
Sheila explaining my interest in Bluefire Inc., then I began searching
for Elaine's publications. I found four. Two were in second-tier
journals, but were at least indexed in our databases. A Google
Scholar search produced two others, published in online open-access
journals. Only one of them was peer-reviewed; the other claimed to
be, but wasn't.

I downloaded them all and sent them to Kevin with an
explanation. He replied, *Thanks. Elias has a list of six articles,
though. You only found four?*

Yeah. Have him send me the list.

A few seconds later an email popped up from Elias. *Here you
go, buckaroo.*

I emailed back, *You are spending WAY too much time with Jon
Eckhoff.*

He responded, *Ha! You got THAT right.*

I chuckled and turned back to Google, using the titles of the
other two articles as my queries. One turned out to be a long entry on
a social psych blog. The other didn't seem to exist. I searched
everywhere I could think of - deep web sites, the Internet Archive. I
sent the link for the blog to Kevin, with a message. *The other one
isn't out there, at least where I can find it. It may have been on a site
that's been shut down.*

OK thx.

I skimmed Elaine's publications and wasn't impressed. She
hadn't done any research of her own. She'd compiled one review
article. The other three articles were closer to pop psychology than
research. The blog post was about the psychology behind multi-level
marketing.

I didn't see how it might relate to her death. But her publication
record provided extra proof that she didn't deserve to be promoted.

Mid-morning Pete texted me as I was on my way to Rosenfeld to see Sheila. *Interview went well. They are doing all interviews today, will let me know by Monday.*

Did they seem impressed with you?

Who knows?

When I got to Sheila's office, she was frowning at her monitor. I said, "Uh oh. I don't like that expression."

"You shouldn't. Bluefire is a shell company."

"Is it illegal?"

"Not necessarily. But it means that the company itself isn't buying the properties near SMC. Someone is using Bluefire as the vehicle for the transactions to maintain their own anonymity."

"Can you find out who's behind it?"

"So far all I'm getting is layers of companies. Bluefire is jointly owned by two separate companies, which themselves seem to be shells."

"Can you tell which one is buying the property?"

"Not yet." She sighed. "Tell Kevin I won't stop digging, but he may end up having to get a subpoena to get to the bottom of it."

"I'll tell him."

I texted Kevin as I walked back to YRL. *Bluefire is a shell company owned by two other shell companies. Sheila says you may need a subpoena.*

Damn. We don't have adequate cause for that yet.

Why do you think it's related to Elaine?

It's not, necessarily. We asked SMC president what board was working on these days, and he mentioned new building complex. May have nothing to do with Elaine. Hence, lack of cause.

Don't give up. Sheila is still working on it.

I never give up, short stuff. :-)

When I got home Pete was banging around in the kitchen. I toed off my shoes and went to kiss him hello - and found that he had all the pots and pans we owned out of the cabinets. "What are you doing?"

"Inventory. We have duplicates of nearly every cooking pot and dish we have. We can take the extras to New Mexico."

"We're not driving there for another two months."

"We can ship them." Pete began replacing some of the pots in the cabinets. "Meredith will have to cook. We'll box up the duplicates and send them to Steve, so they'll be available when Meredith needs them."

Hm. I propped my hip against the counter. "You've been intensely domestic this week. What's going on?"

He frowned at me in confusion. "Whaddya mean, what's going on?"

"You're trying elaborate new recipes; you're sorting through kitchen cabinets - it's all very June Cleaverish."

"You liked the new recipes, right?"

"Of course. That's not what I'm saying."

"What *are* you saying?"

"That this burst of kitchen-based activity is out of character, even for you. It makes me wonder what's swimming around in the recesses of your brain."

He gave an exasperated snort. "Why does it have to *be* anything?"

"It doesn't *have* to be. But try this on for size. Your work life is in turmoil, and you're retreating into this role that strikes me as - housewifely. For lack of a better term."

He stared at me for a minute, his teeth on edge, but I could see the gears working. He picked up a frying pan - for a split second I thought he might whack me with it - then set it aside. "You're right."

"I am?"

"Yeah." He huffed a soft laugh. "I've done this before."

"When?"

"When Uncle Arthur died. I was starting to write my dissertation, I'd just broken up with you, Luke was back - my life was completely discombobulated. I totally reorganized this kitchen. I went through every single cookbook I had, marking recipes. I redecorated the living room." He spread his hands. "I am the product of a repressive heteronormative upbringing, and this is apparently what I do when my life feels out of control."

I waved my hand at the pots and pans. "Did you start this after your interview this morning?"

He laughed weakly. "You've got me figured out, haven't you?"

"Nah." I suspected that would be a lifelong task. "But thanks to my gender-*atypical* upbringing, my recognition of gender-

stereotypical behavior was impaired before I met you. *Now* I have mad skillz."

That made him laugh.

When we were seated and eating Pete asked, "At the risk of sounding like June Cleaver, how was your day?"

I grinned. "Unremarkable, except for my discovery that Elaine never published any original research."

"Her publications were weak?"

"Yep. One review article, a bunch of pop psych and one that turned out to be a blog post."

Pete snorted. "Figures."

"How was *your* day?"

"Unremarkable, except that the entire Board of Trustees showed up in our department today."

I stopped, my fork halfway to my mouth. "*Why?*"

"Since there will be three vacancies, they're going to remodel the department over the summer. It's logical - with three empty offices, they'll only have to maneuver around Curtis, Audra, Elliott and Verlene. I guess they were getting a general idea of how much work was required."

"That must have been awkward."

"Yeah. Fortunately, neither Elliott nor Verlene was around. Only Curtis, Audra and I were there." He huffed a laugh. "I got quite a surprise. I'd just gone down the hall to get a printout from the copier, and when I got back there were these two guys I'd never seen before in my office."

"Did they at least introduce themselves?"

Pete nodded. "William Ostrander and Harold Hendricks."

"They were two of the four who voted for Elaine's reinstatement."

"Yeah. I shook their hands but didn't go out of my way to make them welcome. Of course, we're not supposed to know who voted."

"Did anyone say anything about all of you leaving?"

"Yeah. Most of them were on their way out of the office suite, but one of them hung back. Celine Bachmann. She came into my office, introduced herself, and apologized."

"She wasn't at the emergency meeting. Even if she had been, it wouldn't have made a difference."

"No. But she was still embarrassed by the action. She said she was retired from Pepperdine, so she knows how faculty promotion is supposed to work."

I said, "I don't suppose she had any idea *why* it happened."

"Not that she admitted to me."

We couldn't let Kevin's actual birthday happen without some sort of recognition. At seven, he and Kristen came for ice cream. I said, "Tim let you get away for the evening?"

"Yeah. We've been racking up the overtime so he told us to take tonight off. I do have some good news, though. Of all the other people's fingerprints that *were* in Elaine's house, neither Curtis Glover's nor Audra Rock's were there."

Pete said, "That doesn't mean that they weren't wearing gloves."

"I know. But as of yet there's no evidence tying them to the crime scene."

I asked, "Whose fingerprints *did* you find?"

"Jason Rupp's were all over the bedroom and kitchen. Also two unknowns. Possibly Taylor Vinson's - the other student - and the ex-boyfriend."

Kristen said, "Ahem. Tim said to take the night *off*."

Kevin held up his hands in apology. "I know, I know. That's all I have to say."

Pete said, "I do have to tell you one other thing." He repeated the news about the board's visit to the psychology department.

Kevin frowned. "That sounds legitimate. And they were *all* there."

Kristen said, "It *would* have been suspicious if only one or two of them came."

Pete said, "I agree, it was probably legit. It was awkward, though."

Kevin said, "We're working on setting up interviews with all of them on Sunday. Then they can explain themselves."

Pete said, "All right. We'll stop the cop talk. Now that you two are here, I have something to show you." He opened his laptop. "I recorded a welcome message to use in an online class."

I said, "You're not jumping the gun, are you?"

"Nah. I'll be teaching online *somewhere*, right? I kept it generic. It won't go to waste." He clicked on the video's play arrow.

Pete's smiling face appeared, from the shoulders up. "Hi, everyone. My name's Pete Ferguson, and I'm your instructor this term. Let me tell you a little bit about myself. I grew up in Lancaster, California, in the high desert, and I live in Los Angeles now. I'm a licensed clinical psychologist in the state of California, and I've taught at the college level for seven years. My specialty is abnormal psychology, and I wrote my doctoral dissertation on criminal psychology. I was a patrol officer with the Los Angeles Police Department for ten years before grad school. I'm married, and in my spare time I hike in the Santa Monica Mountains and work in my vegetable garden. And this -" He snapped his fingers, and Ammo appeared on screen, panting with delight - "is my pal Ammo, who's four years old and is a retired Marine bomb-detection dog." Pete flashed a grin at the camera, and I thought, *You just won over all the straight females and gay males in your class.* "I'm looking forward to getting to know all of you. Any time you have a question about anything to do with the class, don't hesitate to ask."

He clicked the *stop* button. "How's that?"

I said, "Very humanizing. Including Ammo was genius."

Kristen said, "That's just right. You gave them enough information to feel like they know you, without actually exposing much."

Kevin said, "So was telling them you were a cop. Maybe they'll think twice about trying to pull anything over on you."

Pete grinned. "They know I'm hundreds of miles away. I doubt that'll deter them."

Saturday, March 25

On Saturday morning we loaded Ammo and the cooler into the CR-V and drove to Ali and Mel's, arriving at the same time as Dad, Jeff, his wife Valerie, and their boys. Jeff, Colin and Gabe donned swim trunks and jumped into the pool with Ammo. Dad caught up with Ali and Mel at poolside while Val and Pete worked in the kitchen.

I couldn't swim or assist with the preparations, so I wandered outside and joined Dad, who was talking to Ali about something to do with Camp Pendleton and her dad. I asked Mel, "How's business?"

"Booming. I'll be glad when Kevin isn't detecting anymore and has extra time for paralegal work."

"He's told you about the social work degree, right?"

"Yeah. It's a terrific fit."

"You're not disappointed that he won't be a full-time paralegal?"

"No. That proposition was mostly for Abby's benefit. It was always difficult for me to imagine Kevin working a full-time desk job."

I said, "I talked to Abby last week. She's going to install built-in shelves and cabinets at the new house later this summer."

Mel was surprised. "Seriously? I didn't know you were still in touch with her."

"I hadn't talked to her for several months, but I told her back then that we hoped she would build for us. Pete and I decided we'd rather pay her than someone we didn't know. And she's building furniture full-time now."

"Ah. I'm glad to hear that it's working out for her. Does Kevin know she's going to work for you?"

"I told him. He didn't seem to care."

Mel grinned. "I like Kristen. I hope she's a keeper."

I grinned back. "I have a good feeling about it."

Kevin, Kristen, Jon and Liz arrived at noon, and Dad and Jon laid burgers on the grill. Kevin, Pete and I ended up applying condiments to our burgers at the same time. Kevin said, "We got all the board interviews lined up for tomorrow. We also tracked down Taylor Vinson, the other student. He's coming in, too. Jon and I - um -"

Pete said, "Let me guess. You want me to sit in the observation room and see if anyone lies about the college."

Kevin grinned. "Would it help if I asked you to do it for my birthday?"

I laughed. Pete said, "You're a pro at making me feel guilty, you know that?"

Kevin looked smug. "Yep."

Colin seated himself between Pete and me and began to eat. I glanced at his plate; he had two burgers and an enormous mound of potato salad. I said, "Hungry?"

He gave me a sideways glance. "I've grown an inch and a half since school started."

Pete asked, "How is school? Still fun?"

"Yeah."

The entire family had been somewhat concerned about Colin's adaptation to high school, after being homeschooled for three years through middle school. We shouldn't have worried. He'd come home at the end of the first week, having joined the Physics Club and the Robotics Club, and as Val said, "He wouldn't shut up about how fantastic school was."

I asked, "Are you coming to Caltech for summer camp this year?" Colin had come to Caltech camps for the past three summers and had roomed with us.

"Yeah. It'll be while you're in Scotland. I'm gonna live with Uncle Kevin and Aunt Kristen."

Pete and I glanced at each other over Colin's head and grinned. "Aunt Kristen" was rapidly becoming both Colin's and Gabe's favorite.

The party was winding down. Jeff was supervising as Colin and Gabe gathered their towels and pool toys. Dad, Val, Ali and Kristen were cleaning up the kitchen. Kevin and I were talking to Mel about the victim advocate system when my phone rang.

It was Sheila Meadows. I said, "Hey, Sheila."

Kevin sat up, his attention piqued. Sheila said, "I hope I'm not interrupting anything."

"Just hanging out at a friend's house. What's up?"

"I had to work today, so I dug back into Bluefire Inc. and found out which of its shells is buying the 16th Street property. It's called Lithian Properties. L-I-T-H-I-A-N."

"Hang on." I entered a note into my phone. "But you said it was a shell company itself, right?"

"Right. The other shell behind Bluefire is Santocean Ltd. But from what I can tell Santocean is in the construction business, not real estate."

"Wonderful. Would you mind emailing what you found to Kevin?"

"On its way. I'll go deeper on Lithian, too."

"Thanks, Sheila." I hung up and said to Kevin, "Now you've got two more company names to throw at the board members tomorrow."

Kevin grinned. "I hate working on the weekends, but I have to say - I'm looking forward to tomorrow."

Sunday, March 26

We arrived at the West LA police station at 7:45 and were ushered into the observation room by Jon. "The LAPD appreciates your assistance, gentlemen."

I said, "Yeah, right. Kevin gets to buy us lunch."

"Of course." Jon grinned. "Best thing about today? I won't have time to spend with my parents."

Pete and I settled in and waited. At 7:59, the door to the interview room opened and Jon appeared, followed by Kevin and an Asian man wearing running garb, whom I assumed to be Zane Wong.

I was right. Jon said politely, "Thanks for meeting with us so early, Mr. Wong."

"Oh, it's no problem. I switched my running route to end up here." Wong smiled. "Although I'm not sure what else I can tell you that we haven't covered already."

Kevin said, "We've learned a few new details that we'd like to ask you about."

Wong was confused. "Concerning Ethicgreen?"

Kevin said, "No, concerning the board of trustees."

"Ah." Wong didn't appear to be surprised. "Ask away."

It seemed that Kevin was going to handle the questioning for Wong. "Tell us again about the emergency meeting on March 10."

Wong nodded. "Augusta Skipper sent out a group email that morning, calling the meeting for that evening. At the time, all she said was that it was concerning a faculty appointment. We'd just approved the promotion list the day before, so I thought maybe someone had been left off."

"Did she say who requested the meeting?"

Wong made a sour face. "No. And no one would admit that at the actual meeting, either. I can't confirm it, but I had the strong impression that the other four had previously decided amongst themselves what they were going to do. Which is not legal."

Kevin said, "I don't suppose they'd be careless enough to leave a trail, if they did?"

Wong scoffed. "No. They wouldn't."

"Why did Celine Bachmann and Charles Mullins miss the meeting?"

"They both had appointments that they couldn't reschedule. Celine had to pick someone up at LAX and Charles had - something."

"When did you find out that the meeting was about Elaine Pareja?"

"When I got there. Augusta called the meeting to order and said that the purpose of the meeting was to vote on reinstatement of a faculty member who'd been wrongfully terminated. I asked who, and she said Elaine's name."

"Then what happened?"

"Someone else - Bill Ostrander, as I recall - asked why Elaine had been terminated. Augusta said it was because she'd been turned down for promotion a third time."

"But you think that Ostrander and the others had discussed Elaine's termination before the meeting."

"Yeah. Bill didn't ask the question as if he was really interested. He asked the question as if he was reading a script."

Kevin leaned back in his seat and crossed his hands over his stomach. "That was the only reason?"

"Yes." Wong was confused again. "Was there another reason?"

Kevin ignored that, as I knew he would. "Did anyone question why Elaine had been turned down for promotion?"

"I did. I asked Augusta if she had Elaine's files. She didn't. I asked her how I was supposed to determine if the termination was wrongful, if I couldn't read the files. She said that Elaine was a vital member of a small department that would be damaged by losing her." Wong leaned forward and tapped a finger firmly on the table. "That's how I knew, later, that they must have arranged it beforehand. No one else at the meeting questioned that. I didn't find out until after Elaine's death - until after I'd talked to you the first time - that most of the department had quit *because* she was reinstated." Wong made a sound of disgust.

"Who told you that?"

"Another faculty member at the college who is an Ethicgreen partner. Alice Greeves. I didn't know Alice well, but after Elaine's death, I called her to see what she knew."

Beside me, Pete made a "huh" sound. Kevin asked Wong, "Do you have any idea who instigated Elaine's reinstatement?"

"No." Wong shook his head. "I'd like to know that myself."

"Okay, Mr. Wong, we're nearly done. What can you tell us about the college's intention to build a new student services center?"

Wong brightened. "Oh, yes. We commissioned a needs assessment about a year ago, and the results clearly indicated that students would benefit from having services consolidated in one area."

"Where will that be built?"

"Well, there isn't a location on campus that works. We've discussed buying property on the west side of campus, across from the stadium, for that purpose."

"But no property has been bought yet?"

"No. We're getting the first funds for that from the state in the coming fiscal year's budget."

Jon asked casually, "Ever heard of the Bluefire Company?"

"No."

"How about Lithian Properties or Santocean Limited?"

Wong shook his head. "No, sorry."

"Just for the record, can you tell us where you were on March 15?"

"I had a rehearsal in the evening." Wong was slightly embarrassed. "I sing with a barbershop quartet, and we rehearse on Wednesdays. After that I went home. My wife and I watched a couple of episodes of *Orange Is the New Black* on Netflix then went to bed."

"All right." Jon glanced at Kevin, who had been taking a few notes and now closed his pen. "Thanks for coming in, Mr. Wong. We apologize for the disruption."

Wong waved that off. "No apology necessary."

Jon saw Wong out and Kevin turned to us, asking through the glass, "Anything?"

Pete hit the *on* button for the intercom. "Alice Greeves said she didn't know Zane Wong well. Wong seemed to confirm that."

"Yup. Wong didn't recognize those companies."

Pete said, "I agree."

Kevin disappeared. Several minutes later, he and Jon returned to the interview room, accompanied by a woman. Probably in her early sixties, cropped white hair, bright blue eyes, wearing a Pepperdine polo shirt and jeans.

Pete turned off the intercom and said, "Celine Bachmann."

"The one that apologized to you."

"Right."

Once again, Kevin did the honors. He said, "Dr. Bachmann, thanks for giving up your morning. We appreciate it."

She smiled. "You're welcome. I'm always glad to have an excuse to come in this direction. It lets me get some shopping done without my husband complaining about unnecessary trips into town."

Jon chuckled. Kevin said, "We'd like to ask you about the emergency board meeting that was called for March 10th."

"Oh." Dr. Bachmann frowned. "I wasn't there."

"Yes, ma'am. How did you find out about the meeting?"

"Augusta Skipper - she's the chair - sent out a group email that morning. I replied immediately - I had to pick up my sister-in-law at the airport at about the same time."

I said, "That matches what Wong said."

Pete said, "Mm hm."

Kevin asked Dr. Bachmann, "When did you find out what happened at the meeting?"

"The next morning. I called Augusta and she told me what they'd done. Reinstating that psychology professor who ended up dead."

"What did you think about that?"

Dr. Bachmann curled her nose. "I thought that stunk. I was on faculty at Pepperdine for eighteen years before I moved into administration there. For a board of trustees to overturn a faculty promotion decision is almost unheard of. I asked Augusta what the hell they'd been thinking, and she spouted some crap line about the psych department not being able to do without her. I pointed out that it would have been the psych department that *turned her down* for promotion three times, but she wasn't interested in what I thought."

"How did that seem to you?"

Dr. Bachmann gave Kevin a knowing look. "Does it seem like there must have been some other reason? Of course. Do I have any idea what that might be? None. I wish I did."

"Any theories?"

She laughed. "Not interested in just the facts, ma'am? No, I don't have any theories. Augusta clearly lied, though, because I learned after Ms. Pareja's death that half the psych department ended up quitting because of her reinstatement. And I don't blame them. I apologized to one of them last week."

Beside me, Pete smiled. Kevin asked, "Do you know Mrs. Skipper well?"

"No. She and I don't run in the same circles. Augusta lives in one of those gigantic houses on the beach that's going to fall into the ocean with the next severe storm. She's the type whose living room appears in House Beautiful while her kids are snorting coke in the media room."

Jon made a note. Kevin asked, "Have Ms. Skipper's children been in legal trouble?"

"No. They're rich white kids, so they've been to rehab instead."

"I see. Any idea who might have wanted Elaine Pareja dead?"

"No. Unless it was someone who'd be forced to work with her." Dr. Bachmann snorted. "Sorry, that was a cheap joke. I didn't know Ms. Pareja at all."

Pete sighed. I knew he was remembering Curtis's lack of alibi. Jon asked, "Does the name Bluefire Company mean anything to you?"

Dr. Bachmann was puzzled. "No."

"What about a company named Lithian?"

"Lithi*um?*"

"No, Lithian. With an AN."

"What an odd word. No, I've not heard of that one."

"Santocean Limited?"

"No." Dr. Bachmann appeared as if she wanted to ask what the companies were, but knew she wouldn't get an answer.

"Where were you on the night of March 15?"

Dr. Bachmann smiled. "Catalina Island. My husband and I spent last week there with our daughter and son-in-law."

Once again, Kevin and Jon seemed to exchange some sort of silent signal. Kevin handed one of his cards across the table. "Okay, Dr. Bachmann, thank you again. If anything else occurs to you that might be useful, no matter how trivial, please let me know."

"I will."

Jon saw Dr. Bachmann out while Kevin conferred with us. "Everything right about that?"

Pete said, "Yes. It was me she apologized to. And I believe her about the companies, too."

I said, "I'll be curious to hear what Augusta Skipper has to say about the psych department."

Kevin snorted. "You're not the only one. You guys need a break?"

Pete and I both visited the men's room, then returned to our post. A minute later, Kevin and Jon led Charles Mullins into the interview room.

I remembered that Mullins was a retired Air Force brigadier general, and he had a military bearing. Ramrod-straight posture, nearly-shaved head, suit and tie. Kevin introduced himself and Jon and said, "We appreciate you coming in on a Sunday morning, sir."

Mullins nodded sharply at Kevin. "Not a problem. Went to sunrise service this morning. How can I help you?"

"What can you tell us about the emergency board of trustees meeting called for Friday, March 10th?"

"Very little. I couldn't be there. An airman who served under me had passed, and his funeral was being held at the same time, at the National Cemetery up by UCLA. His name was Ricardo Quezada, if you want to check."

Jon wrote down the name, but I suspected it would check out. I figured that if I looked up *straightforward* in the dictionary, General Mullins's picture would be there. Kevin said, "Thank you, sir. Did you find out later what had occurred at the meeting?"

"Yes, I did. Sent Bill Ostrander an email that evening, asking him what went on. He said they'd reinstated a faculty member."

"Did he tell you why?"

"He said she'd been wrongly turned down for promotion by her department." Mullins gave Kevin a narrow stare. "Was that not the case?"

Kevin turned it back around. "Did *you* have any reason to believe that might not be the case?"

"Not at the time, no." Mullins crossed his arms. "You're telling me there was something wrong with that?"

Kevin said, "Let me tell you this. Elaine Pareja was a member of the psychology department. Her own department had turned her down for promotion three times. That decision was reversed by the board, by a vote of 4-1. Skipper, Ostrander, Barrientos and Hendricks voted for reinstatement, and Zane Wong voted against. Any thoughts?"

Mullins tapped his chin, thoughtfully regarding Kevin. "Skipper, Barrientos and Hendricks form a voting bloc more often than not. Ostrander doesn't always go along."

I said to Pete, "Those three are all involved in the property business to some extent."

Pete said, "Maybe you should send your friend Sheila their names."

In the interview room Kevin was asking, "What can you tell us about the college's intention to buy property along 16th Street?"

Mullins's narrow stare was back. "That it's still in the discussion stages. The legislature has provided some funding in next year's budget."

Property deals... I pulled out my phone and texted Sheila. *Three names for you: Augusta Skipper, Hardhat Holdings. Harold Hendricks, Santa Monica hotelier. Sierra Barrientos, attorney with Dawson, Duncan and Hill. If you would, check to see if there are any connections between them, or any connections with them and your shell companies. Thanks!! I owe you!*

Jon asked Mullins about the companies; he'd never heard of any of them. His alibi was that he'd attended a three-day conference for church elders in Denver. Kevin gave Mullins his card, and Jon walked him out. When Pete turned on the intercom I said, "Property deals. You've got a developer's wife, a hotel guy, and a real estate lawyer there. Sounds fishy to me."

Kevin said, "Me, too. Not sure how the judge fits in yet."

Pete said, "Maybe he's the connection to Elaine."

Kevin scratched his head. "Maybe. When he comes in, we'll ask him."

I said, "Is he next?"

"Nope. The next name on the dance card is Augusta Skipper herself."

Pete said, "I can't *wait* to hear her explanation for Elaine's reinstatement."

Kevin grinned. "Neither can I. Jon gets to lay the charm on our four problem children."

I said, "What are you gonna do?"

Pete said, "He's going to sit there and look dangerous."

Kevin just laughed.

Augusta Skipper looked like someone whose living room would be in House Beautiful. She was wearing pristinely white tennis clothes that didn't appear to have ever been sweated in. Jon introduced Kevin and himself, and immediately started laying it on. "Thank you for coming in this morning, Mrs. Skipper. We really appreciate it."

Augusta fluffed her hair. "Oh, it's quite all right. I'm a huge supporter of law enforcement."

Pete snorted. Jon said, "That means a lot to us. Mrs. Skipper, I'd like to ask you some questions about your service on the Santa Monica College Board of Trustees."

Augusta fluffed her hair again. "Of course. How can I help you?"

Pete said, "That hair-fluffing thing must be a tell for her."

"Think she's nervous?"

"Oh, yeah."

Jon was asking Augusta, "How long have you been chair of the board?"

"Nine months. Our terms run for two years."

"So the chairship will move to someone else in July 2018?"

"That's right."

Jon smiled. "Tell me about what the board is working on these days."

"We're going to renovate some of the worn-out faculty offices on campus. We'll probably request bids in early fall."

"Ah. What departments?"

Augusta looked confused, as if she couldn't imagine why Jon was asking about this, but her stated admiration for law enforcement wouldn't allow her to question him. "For now, those in the Humanities and Social Sciences building."

"I see. Remind me what departments are included in Humanities and Social Sciences?"

Augusta's gaze flickered to Kevin for a split second. He was sitting at a diagonal to her, his arms crossed, watching her without moving. She said, "I believe there's history, sociology, geography…" She counted on her fingers. "Let's see, there were five. History, sociology, geography - oh! Economics. And - ah - psychology."

Pete laughed. Jon said, "Psychology too?"

"Yes." Augusta's eyes flicked to Kevin again.

"Okay, so you've got an office renovation project coming up. Does the board have other projects in the works?"

"We're strategizing for a new student services building. To consolidate all the services in one location."

"Oh? Where will that go?"

"We haven't nailed down the location yet."

I said to Pete, "There's a discrepancy."

"Yup."

Jon took off his sport coat and draped it over the back of his chair, ensuring that Augusta had a close-up view of his shoulder holster. "I see. Tell me about the emergency meeting you called on March 10."

Pete murmured, "Damn, he's getting good at this."

Augusta was flustered. "Emergency meeting? Oh - yes. I remember. We had to reinstate a faculty member who'd been wrongly terminated."

"What was his or her name?"

"Elaine Pareja."

"Why had she been terminated?"

Augusta fluffed her hair. "There was a vendetta against her in the psychology department. She'd been wrongly denied promotion, and the administration had let her go. We reinstated her."

"How do you know her promotion was wrongly denied?"

"Well, ah -"

"Did you examine her paperwork? Did you read her HR file? Did you ask the chair of the psychology department why she'd been released? Did you consult with the academic dean?"

Augusta blinked. "No."

"Why not?"

"We didn't believe it was necessary."

Kevin snorted. Augusta shot him a grimace laced with near-panic. Jon asked, "Who told you it wasn't necessary?"

Augusta decided to get haughty. "*Really*, Detective. We had it on good authority that the faculty member in question was *fully* qualified for her position. We wouldn't have reinstated her otherwise."

Kevin had been balancing his chair on its back two legs; now he lowered it with a thump. "On *whose* good authority, Mrs. Skipper?"

Augusta stared at Kevin. "Another faculty member in the psychology department."

"Which one?"

"Oh - what *was* the name?"

Kevin laughed. Jon said, "Mrs. Skipper, there are only four of them. What was the name?"

Augusta set her jaw. "Audra Rock."

I said, "I thought Elaine and Audra didn't like each other."

"They didn't. Audra would never have said *anything* to get Elaine reinstated."

Jon said, "We've questioned Dr. Rock. She said she did no such thing."

That was Augusta's story, and she was sticking to it. "Well. That's not consistent with what she told *me*."

"Uh huh." Jon leaned forward, completely abandoning the "good cop" role. "See, here's the thing, Mrs. Skipper. We've seen Elaine's application and files, and we've spoken to everyone in the psychology department. Elaine was a low-performing faculty member with poor evaluations and a lousy attitude. But that's not nearly as relevant as the fact that she was sleeping with at least two of her students, which is expressly stated in the faculty handbook as being grounds for dismissal. Her 'wrongful termination' was instead exactly the *right* thing to do. So that creates *overwhelming* curiosity in us. What was the *real* reason she was reinstated?"

Augusta was gritting her teeth. "She was sleeping with a student? We had *no* idea."

Kevin made a "pfft" sound. Jon sighed. "Mrs. Skipper. You can tell us the truth now, or you can tell us under oath when Elaine's murderer goes to trial. But you *will* tell us."

I could see the wheels turning in Augusta's brain. Pete said, "Whatever she says next is gonna be a corker."

Augusta spoke slowly, seemingly choosing her words with care. "We were approached by a third party who felt that it was vital that Ms. Pareja remain with the college."

"Who was this third party?"

"I don't know." Augusta lifted her chin in defiance, but ruined the effect by fluffing her hair.

"You were approached, but you don't know by whom?"

"The person wished to remain anonymous."

"And you blindly took the word of this anonymous person that Elaine had to be reinstated?"

Augusta had to realize she was trapped, but she was determined to sink with the boat she'd sailed in on. "Yes."

Kevin shook his head. Jon said, "Ever hear of Bluefire Company?"

Augusta's eyes widened as the rest of her body froze. "No."

"Lithian Holdings?"

"No."

"Santocean Limited?"

"No." But Augusta was sweating. I could see the pulse pounding in her neck.

Pete said, "That woman's pants are *incendiary.*"

"Where were you on the night of March 15?"

"At home."

"Alone?"

"With my husband." Who, I bet, would support her alibi regardless of whether she'd been home or not.

Jon and Kevin looked at each other. Jon grinned. Kevin rolled his eyes and made a dismissive gesture with his hand. Jon had a stack of file folders in front of him; he straightened them, seemingly holding back laughter. "Okay, Mrs. Skipper. That's all."

Augusta didn't believe it. "That's all?"

"Yes, ma'am. You're free to go." Jon stood up and held the door for her. "Have a nice day. We'll talk again. *Soon.*"

"Er - very well." Augusta left, with one fleeting glance at Kevin as she went out the door.

Kevin stood up and stretched. "What a load of bullshit."

Pete re-activated the intercom. "That statement she made about a third party? That wasn't entirely BS. *Someone* felt it was vital that Elaine be reinstated. I doubt very seriously that it was a third party, though."

Jon said, "There was no third party. It was one of them."

Kevin said, "Elaine knew something. She had information that allowed her to force her way back into her job - but then somehow that same information got her killed. My gut says it's this land deal, but we don't have the evidence yet."

I said, "I sent Sheila the names of the three board members and their companies. She'll resume the hunt tomorrow."

Pete asked, "Who's next?"

Jon checked his notes. "Sierra Barrientos, real estate attorney. Then we eat lunch."

My first reaction when Sierra Barrientos walked into the room was, *Uh-oh*. Augusta had been manipulatable, possibly believing that she was made immune from suspicion by her money. I was sure that Sierra held no such delusions - and was highly unlikely to fall for any interrogative tricks.

Jon didn't even venture it. "Dr. Barrientos, thanks for coming in."

Sierra raised an eyebrow. "*Dr.* Barrientos?"

Anyone who didn't know Jon would miss the touch of snark in his tone. "Oh, my mistake. I thought you were a J.D."

"Ah. So I am." She was amused. "You can call me Sierra."

"All right, Sierra." Jon crossed his forearms on the table. "As I'm sure you know, we're investigating the death of Elaine Pareja."

"Yes."

"Were you acquainted with Ms. Pareja?"

"No."

I said, "She's answering questions as if she's on the witness stand."

Pete nodded. "We won't get any spontaneous information out of this one."

"Tell me about the emergency board meeting of Friday, March 10."

Sierra shrugged slightly. "Augusta Skipper sent out an email calling a meeting. When we got there, she said a faculty member - Elaine Pareja from psychology - had been wrongly terminated and we needed to reinstate her."

"Was there any discussion before the vote?"

"A little. Zane Wong wanted to see the files. Augusta said she didn't have them."

"Didn't that seem odd?"

Another shrug. "What can I tell you? Augusta isn't a detail-oriented person."

"What reason did Mrs. Skipper provide for the wrongful termination?"

"That Ms. Pareja was let go after a third application for promotion was turned down."

Jon tapped the tips of his fingers together. "What reason did Mrs. Skipper have to justify reinstating Ms. Pareja?"

"That the psychology department couldn't do without her."

"Are you aware of how the promotion process works at SMC?"

Sierra was insulted. "Of course."

"Then you know that it was the psychology department who denied her promotion. *They* didn't think they needed her."

"I trusted that Augusta had done her due diligence."

"And yet you said she wasn't a detail-oriented person."

Sierra sighed. "Detective. I happen to believe that it's inappropriate to rob someone of their livelihood for questionable cause. We weren't voting to *promote* Ms. Pareja. We only voted to hand her current job back to her."

Kevin was watching Sierra closer than he had Augusta. He hadn't moved at all since she'd entered the room, and she hadn't looked his way. I said, "Sierra's not worried about Kevin like Augusta was."

Pete chuckled. "That may be a mistake. She's only a real estate lawyer, after all."

A real estate lawyer... It occurred to me that one of Mel's best friends, Tasha Jimenez, was a real estate attorney. I made a mental note to remind Kevin.

In the interview room Jon said, "Ms. Pareja wasn't terminated because of her poor evaluation."

Sierra didn't bat an eye. "No?"

"No. You weren't aware that she'd been sleeping with her students?"

Sierra fixed Jon with a stare. "No, I was not."

Pete said, "Hm."

Jon said, "If you had, would you have switched your vote?"

"Of *course*." Sierra glared at him.

Kevin said, "Tell us about the land deal."

Sierra's head turned toward Kevin slowly. "Land deal?"

"Along 16th Street."

"Ah." Another shrug. "The college is studying the potential building of a new student services complex there."

"Is your law firm involved in that?"

Sierra's voice was icily calm. "Of course not. That would be a conflict of interest."

"Is Hardhat Holdings involved in the land deal?"

Sierra reminded me of a rattlesnake, unblinking eyes measuring her adversary. "That would also be a conflict of interest."

"Yes, it would. That's not what I asked you."

"I'm not aware that Hardhat is involved in any way."

Pete said, "She's considering throwing Augusta under the bus. But she's not going to do it yet."

Kevin asked, "Mrs. Skipper told us that Ms. Pareja's reinstatement was instigated by a third party. Any idea who that was?"

Sierra said evenly, "As far as I knew, the reinstatement was instigated by Augusta herself."

Pete said, "Aaaaand she just changed her mind."

Kevin had a tiny smile playing around his mouth. Sierra narrowed her eyes a bit but didn't say anything. Jon said, "Four more questions. Ever heard of Bluefire Company?"

Sierra's expression didn't vary. "No."

"Lithian Holdings?"

"No."

"Santocean Limited?"

"No." But I thought I saw a fleeting twitch on Sierra's face.

"Where were you on the night of Elaine's murder?"

Sierra gave Jon a challenging sneer. "You'll have to remind me of the date."

Pete muttered, "She's smart."

Jon said, "March 15."

"May I consult my calendar?"

"Of course."

Sierra took out her phone. "I worked late at the office that night, then went home."

"Alone?"

"Yes."

Jon smiled. "All right. We appreciate your cooperation, Sierra. You're free to go. We'll probably have additional questions later."

Sierra said, "I'll look forward to it." She opened the door for herself and left.

Jon tapped on our window. "Chinese food okay for lunch? The taco truck isn't here on the weekends."

Kevin and I stepped into the hallway simultaneously. I said, "Chinese food is fine."

Kevin took our orders and left. Jon said, "What did you think?"

Pete shook his head. "She's slick."

"No shit. She's a lawyer." Jon led the way to his desk, in the corner of the detectives' room. "She said her law firm wasn't involved in the deal. That may be technically true. They're not involved *yet*."

I said, "Likewise, Hardhat Holdings."

Pete said, "She doesn't like Augusta much. And she *has* heard of Santocean. Although she might have been telling the truth about the other two companies."

Jon agreed. "She wants to pin Elaine's reinstatement on Augusta."

Pete said, "She might be right."

As we ate Kevin called Mel's friend, Tasha Jimenez. When she answered he said, "Hi, Tasha, it's Kevin Brodie. I hate to bother you on a weekend." He chuckled. "Are you? What a coincidence. I'm at work too. Just a quick question. In the course of our current investigation, we turned up the name of a real estate attorney in Santa Monica named Sierra Barrientos. Do you know her?" He listened for a moment, interest spreading across his face. "No kidding. Is she a partner? Ah. Is she good at it? No, she's not in any trouble at all." He held up two crossed fingers, at which Jon snickered. "The Santa Monica College faculty member that was found murdered in her home. Sierra's on the college board of trustees. Right now she's just a name on the list. You bet. Thanks, Tasha."

He hung up. "Sierra is the rainmaker for Dawson, Duncan and Hill. She's not a partner."

I asked, "What's a rainmaker?"

"The person in the firm who's primarily responsible for drumming up business."

Pete said, "Which would be real estate transactions. Land deals."

Kevin pointed his chopsticks at Pete. "Precisely."

Thirty minutes later we were back in the observation room, watching as Jon introduced himself and Kevin to Judge William Ostrander. I said to Pete, "Another lawyer."

"Yeah."

Ostrander looked as if he'd just come from the golf course. Jon approached him in the same fashion as he had Sierra Barrientos - and he repeated nearly the same story. His reasoning for Elaine's reinstatement was the same as Sierra's - nearly word for word.

I said, "They've *rehearsed* this."

Ostrander was shocked - *shocked* - to learn that Elaine had been sleeping with a student. He wasn't as convincing as Sierra. Kevin and Jon let it show on their faces that they didn't believe him, but didn't press him on it.

He also flatly denied having ever met Elaine.

Kevin asked, "Tell us about the land deal."

"Land deal? Oh, you mean for the new student services building?"

"Yes, sir."

"There *aren't* any deals yet. We've been examining architectural drawings, but we haven't had any money to buy property with. Come July 1 there *will* be some land deals."

"Any chance Hardhat will get a piece of that action?"

Ostrander laughed. "They'd better not. No - Augusta isn't the brightest bulb in the pack, but her husband's a smart guy. He wouldn't bid for that deal."

Jon said, "We understand that the available property along 16th Street is primarily owned by a company called Bluefire. Ever heard of it?"

Ostrander, like Augusta, went very still, but he was skilled at extricating himself from it. "No. But like I said, the college hasn't moved to buy any of those properties yet."

"What about Lithian Holdings?"

Ostrander struck an earnest expression. "It's not familiar to me."

"Santocean Limited?"

Ostrander's expression didn't flicker. "No."

Ostrander's alibi was that he was home with his wife. No stronger than Augusta's. Kevin dismissed him, and we conferred via intercom. Jon said, "I don't get why Ostrander voted for Elaine. Just because Augusta wanted him to? No way. And he doesn't have an obvious connection to the property business."

Pete said, "He's heard of those companies, though. And he and Augusta both were *quite* surprised that you mentioned them."

Kevin was wearing his snarly expression. "I *hate* being lied to by a judge."

Jon said, "Maybe the other board members only need him for his vote."

I said, "Even if he'd voted against Elaine, it still would have been 3-2. Maybe he knew that and didn't want to create enemies."

"Possible." Kevin sighed. "Okay. Two more, then we're done."

The first word that sprang to mind when I saw Harold Hendricks was *smarmy*. I said, "This is the other guy you found in your office?"

"Yeah."

"He seems - unlikeable."

Pete snorted. "He resembles a hit man Kev and I arrested once."

"Any relation?"

"Nah. That guy's name was something Russian."

Jon asked, "You're in the hotel business, Mr. Hendricks?"

"Yes. I own three hotels here in town." He named three upscale hotels near the beach.

"Have you owned them long?"

"Fifteen to twenty years."

Jon nodded. "I expect you do well in those locations."

Hendricks's smile was oily. "I do."

Jon apparently decided to take a shot in the dark. "How did you know Elaine Pareja?"

Hendricks sighed. "Ah, poor Elaine. I met her about two years ago at a college function - a scholarship fundraiser. We sat at the same table and struck up a conversation."

"Were you friends?"

"Friendly acquaintances, more like."

I asked Pete, "How did Jon know that?"

Pete shook his head. "I doubt that he did. No one else admitted knowing her, so he took a shot, hoping he'd hit something."

I said, "Bullseye."

"Yup."

In the interview room Jon was asking, "When was the last time you saw her?"

Hendricks thought - or appeared to do so. "It was at least a year ago. She was having dinner at one of my hotels with a gentleman friend."

Pete said, "Lie."

Jon asked, "Did she introduce her friend?"

"It was the same man she'd been with at the scholarship dinner. I can't remember his name."

"Were you responsible for getting her reinstated to the college?"

Hendricks seemed to be surprised. "No, that was Augusta Skipper's doing."

"How so?"

Hendricks spread his hands. "Augusta called the meeting. I assumed it was her idea."

"Did you know about the issues Elaine was having in the psychology department?"

"Issues? No. Augusta said the other faculty members held a grudge against her. I didn't know anything about it."

"Would it surprise you to learn that she was sleeping with at least two of her students?"

Hendricks's jaw dropped a bit too much to be believable. "*No.* Are you serious?"

"Yes, sir. No one on the board brought that up at any time?"

"Absolutely not. Believe me, Detective, if I'd had *any* idea…"

Pete muttered, "Yeah, right."

Jon asked Hendricks about the land deal; his response was identical to Judge Ostrander's. I said, "Is that another thing they've practiced?"

Pete said, "Sounds like it to me."

Kevin spoke up. "Mr. Hendricks, do you have any idea who might have wanted to harm Elaine?"

"No." Hendricks shook his head. "Could it have been related to those two students?"

Pete snickered. Kevin said blandly, "At this point we're entertaining all possibilities."

Jon said, "One last thing. Have you ever heard of a company called Bluefire?"

Hendricks's élan evaporated. "Ah - well, now, I believe I have. Couldn't tell you where I've come across it, though."

"What about Lithian Holdings?"

Hendricks paled, and he adjusted the pleats of his golf pants. "I'm not sure. It's vaguely familiar."

"Santocean Limited?"

"That's also familiar."

Jon flicked a glance at Kevin, who said, "Where were you on March 15?"

Hendricks shook his head. "Home, alone. And yes, I know how that appears."

Kevin said, "Yes, sir. Thank you for coming in, Mr. Hendricks. We may have additional questions in the future."

"Of course. You know where to find me."

When Hendricks was gone, Pete said via intercom, "He's familiar with Lithian and Santocean, all right. And it was interesting, what he said about Elaine's death being related to the students, *and* I'd bet he's seen Elaine more recently than one year ago."

Kevin said, "He may suspect something about the student angle and hopes we'll turn in that direction."

I said, "To stop you from investigating those companies?"

Jon grinned. "At this point, Dr. Brodie, we're entertaining all possibilities."

I laughed. Kevin said, "Let's see if Elaine's student will tell us anything."

When Taylor Vinson walked into the interview room, Pete and I simultaneously said, "*Whoa.*"

Taylor was an Adonis. Curly dark hair, long-lashed eyes, broad shoulders, narrow waist, gorgeous ass. He was wearing board shorts, a tank top and flip-flops. I said, "*What* sport does this guy play?"

"Water polo. *Damn.*"

"Maybe we should start attending their games."

"Mm *hm.*" Pete moved a little closer to the glass. "He reminds me of someone."

"He took psychology classes. Maybe you've seen him in the department."

"Maybe. Pretty sure I'd remember *him*, though."

"He's memorable, all right."

Jon said, "Thanks for coming in, Mr. Vinson."

Then Taylor opened his mouth and ruined the illusion. "Yeah, like, whatever."

I groaned. Pete said, "He did get a C minus from Aaron…"

Jon said, "Tell us about Elaine Pareja."

Taylor shrugged. "Elaine was cool."

"How so?"

"I don't know. She was, like…cool. 'Specially for an old lady. She listened to cool music and shit."

I snickered. Jon said, "How did you meet her?"

"In class. She was my teacher for - uh - sociology psych this semester."

I said, "Sociology psych?"

Pete said, "Yeah, like, whatever."

I laughed. Jon asked, "How did you end up sleeping with her?"

Taylor shrugged. "I, like, fuckin' *bombed* my first test. I asked Elaine if there was anything I could do for extra credit." He smirked. "She said yes."

"What happened then?"

"She gave me her address and said to come over that evening. We ate pizza and smoked some weed and then we, like, got it on. You know."

Pete muttered, "Dear God."

Jon said, "Did you spend the night?"

"Nah. It wasn't like that. We were just hooking up, you know? Besides, Coach does bed checks."

"Ah. You live in student housing?"

"Sort of. There's apartment buildings across from campus. The athletes live there."

"All right. So Elaine altered your test grade?"

"Nah. She made a category for extra credit and gave me points there."

"Was she giving anyone else this sort of extra credit?"

Taylor smirked again. "I heard there was another guy the semester before me. That's why I asked her for it."

Pete sighed. "How did we not hear these rumors?"

I said, "Alice Greeves heard them. And your librarian, Annie Snow. Maybe it was a female grapevine thing."

Jon asked, "How long did it last? You and Elaine hooking up?"

"Until she died." Taylor frowned. "That was, like, a total kick in the head, you know?"

"When was the last time you were with her?"

"Uh -" Taylor gazed at the ceiling, his mouth gaping, apparently exercising his little gray cells. "It was right before she got fired. The other guy she was doing turned out to be the one killed in that street racing accident, right? It was the night before that accident."

"Tuesday, March 7th?"

"Uh - yeah, it was a Tuesday. We watched *NCIS* while we were - um - toking."

"Did Elaine say anything to you about that accident? Or the other student?"

"Nah. I didn't talk to her after that happened. We were s'posed to get together on Thursday but she texted me to cancel. I texted her a couple of times after that but she didn't get back to me, you know? I figured she was just blowing me off." Taylor shrugged. "Or she mighta, like, found another student that needed extra credit."

"How did you find out about the student who was killed, then?"

Taylor looked cagey. "Somebody else said so."

"Who?"

"A guy I know. I mean, I don't know his name."

"Is he an SMC student?"

"Yeah. He hangs out at The Daily Pint." A bar not too far from campus.

Jon smiled. "How old are you, Taylor?"

He made a "duh" face. "Nineteen. So?"

"Do you have any idea who might have killed Elaine?"

Taylor was surprised. "Dude, no *way*. I'd tell if I did."

"Did she say *anything* to you about anyone she was having trouble with?"

"Nah. She bitched about the other psych professors, but that was just, like, whining." Taylor laughed. "She said they didn't respect her. I thought, *duh*, lady, you're the one fuckin' a student. But I didn't *say* that. I didn't wanna turn off the faucet, you know what I mean?"

Pete snickered. Jon said, "I know what you mean. Did she supply the weed?"

"Yeah. She always had it there." Taylor's eyebrows went up. "Maybe it was a drug deal gone south?"

Pete said, "Hm."

Jon said, "At this point, we're not ruling anything out. I don't suppose you have any idea where she got the weed?"

"Nope. Didn't wanna know. It was good shit, though." Taylor held up his hands. "I don't have any, I swear."

Jon grinned. "Relax. We're not interested in busting you for that. Let me ask you this. Have you ever heard of a company called Bluefire?"

"Yeah. I think so."

Jon and Kevin both sat up straighter. Jon asked, "Do you remember where?"

"Lemme think." Taylor appealed to the ceiling again. "Uh - Elaine mighta mentioned it."

Pete blew out a breath. I was frozen in place. Jon asked, "When was this?"

"Uh - the last time I saw her."

"Do you remember what she was talking about at the time?"

"She wasn't talking to me. She was on the phone. Dunno to who."

"Was it someone she called, or someone who called her?"

"They called her."

"Did she say a name?"

"Don't think so." Taylor shrugged. "I was kinda stoned, you know?"

Jon said, "Are you sure you remember the name?"

"Oh, yeah. She said, 'Bluefire,' and I thought, 'Dude, that is a *sick* word.' Sounded like a cool name for a surfboard company or something."

"Could you hear a voice on the other end? Was she talking to a man or a woman?"

"I couldn't hear."

Kevin said, "Are you a local boy, Taylor?"

"Yeah. Went to the Brentwood School."

"Were you raised in Brentwood?"

"Nah. In Santa Monica."

"Who are your parents?"

Taylor rolled his eyes. "Lawyers. They're divorced, since I was seven. Me and my brother lived with our dad and stepmom."

"What kind of law do your parents practice?"

"Don't worry. They're not gonna sue you because I talked to you. At least, my dad won't. My mom's a bitch. But we don't get along, so you're probably safe."

Pete said, "Wow."

Kevin smiled. "I'm not worried. Just curious."

"My dad's an entertainment lawyer and my mom's a real estate lawyer. They're not, like, famous."

Real estate? Kevin said, "I run into a lot of lawyers when I have to testify in court. Maybe I know them."

Taylor shrugged. "Gregory Vinson and Sierra Barrientos."

Pete and I both sucked in breaths. Kevin and Jon didn't twitch. Kevin said, "You're right. I don't know them."

Taylor seemed worried. "You're not, like, gonna call 'em or anything, right?"

Jon smiled. "No. You're technically an adult."

"Yeah." Taylor's tone was indignant. "What's up with that? I can vote and kill terrorists, but I'm not supposed to drink? *Dude.*"

Jon said, "We don't write the laws. We just enforce them."

"Yeah, whatever." Taylor squirmed. "Are we about done? I've got study hall at five."

Kevin said, "Almost done. Did your parents know you were involved with Elaine?"

"My mom found out. She pays for my phone, so she says she can go through it any time she wants. I had to get a ride from her, and she made me pump gas so she could search my phone." Taylor grimaced. "I thought I'd erased all of Elaine's texts. Guess I missed a couple."

"And where were you on the night Elaine was killed?"

"At my apartment. You can ask Coach."

"All right." Kevin slid a card across the table. "If you remember anything else, you let me know."

"Sure." Taylor pocketed the card and stood up. "Can I go?"

Jon stood and opened the door. "Thanks for coming in."

Taylor disappeared. I counted to ten then entered the hallway. "Elaine knew something about Bluefire."

Jon said, "Yep. And Harold Hendricks admitted knowing her, *and* he recognized both Bluefire and Lithian. We have to confront him."

Pete said, "Elaine was screwing *Sierra's kid*. And Sierra knew it."

Kevin said, "How about that? We'll have to confront Sierra, too."

I said, "What made you ask him that?"

"I thought he looked like her, especially through the eyes." He grinned. "I was right."

Pete said, "Damn. *That's* who he reminded me of."

Jon said, "You two are probably over this."

I said, "And we've got a dog at home with his legs crossed."

Kevin laughed. "We've got people to call. Jamie, I'll talk to you tomorrow about what Sheila finds."

"Yep."

As we walked home I said, "What do you think now? Was Elaine killed because of the board, or because of her indiscretions?"

Pete sighed. "I'm still betting that her death was related to the land deal, especially since she knew something about Bluefire. I can't imagine killing someone for having sex with your adult son. Elaine's reinstatement had to be related to the land deal too. If she knew something about the land deal, and she got her job back - whoever might be harmed by her knowledge of the property issue might have decided that she was too much trouble."

"But then why would that person have voted to reinstate her?"

"Because then he or she would have exposed himself or herself. I don't believe all four of them were in on Elaine's death. I bet only one of them was, and he or she couldn't tell the others why."

"Or it might have been her drug dealer."

"Yeah. That too."

When we got home Ammo dashed into the front yard and took a long pee against the front edge of one of Pete's raised beds. I said, "Ammo's been cooped up all day, and so have we. Why don't we walk him down around your campus? Specifically, along 16th Street?"

Pete grinned. "Casing the neighborhood?"

"Why not?"

We parked at Pete's building and walked across campus to 16th Street. The neighborhood across from the stadium consisted of three streets - Bay, Grant, and Pacific - bordered by 16th Street on the east and 14th Street on the west. Bay, Grant and Pacific all dead-ended just before 16th, but there were walkways that crossed from the ends of Bay and Grant to pedestrian crossings on 16th leading to campus.

Pete and I crossed onto Grant Street and began to stroll. It was an aging neighborhood. The trees lining the street were enormous, and the houses were modest but neatly kept. A couple of houses appeared to be empty, and I pointed them out to Pete. "Want to bet Bluefire owns those?"

"You should write down the addresses. We can check the county assessor's site."

I took out my phone and made notes. "Some of these others must be rentals."

"Yeah, but it's impossible to tell which."

We got to the intersection of 14th Street and stopped. I said, "What happened to 15th Street?"

"Eh. The numbering gets screwy on this side of Pico."

We turned left and walked up Pacific. There were three empty houses toward the campus end of the street, and I made a note of the addresses. Where the street dead-ended, an elderly man was working in the yard. He glanced up at us, frowning, but then smiled when he saw Ammo. "Handsome dog."

Pete said, "Thank you. His name's Ammo."

The man held out his hand. Ammo sniffed it, then allowed his ears to be scratched. The man chuckled. "He likes that."

Pete said, "Oh, yeah."

"You fellas don't live on this street."

Pete said, "No, sir. I teach at the college. We come down here to walk sometimes."

I'd been observing the man's house, and had noticed something. "Do you mind if I ask - what's the Not for Sale sign for?"

The man turned and looked at his sign, which was displayed prominently on a stake by his front walk. "Just what it says. You're from the college, you say?"

Pete said, "I am."

"Then you should know. They want all this property for some new building."

Pete said, "I've just begun to hear about that. Faculty are always the last to know anything. Has someone been after you to sell?"

The man nodded. "We've had a couple of people approach us. Offering crazy amounts of money for this place. Lots of the neighbors have accepted the deal."

I said, "I noticed a couple of empty houses back that way, and over on Grant."

"Yep." The man waved at the houses across the street. "A bunch of these others are rentals, and the folks have been informed that their leases won't be renewed. They'll all be out by December."

Pete said, "This is a great neighborhood. I don't blame you for not moving."

"Lived here fifty years." He pointed to a large tree in his front yard. "Planted that as a sapling when my first boy was born, 47 years ago. My wife has some health difficulties now, and we've got this house fixed up just to suit her. We're not leaving."

I said, "Good for you."

The man frowned again. "You're not spies for the college, are you?"

Pete laughed. "No, sir. I promise you that. My name's Pete Ferguson and I teach in the psychology department. You can look me up if you want."

I said, "I work at UCLA. He's my only connection to the college."

"That's all right then, I guess." But the man still seemed suspicious. I didn't blame him.

Pete asked, "Do you have other neighbors that are refusing to sell?"

"Yup. There are six of us that are holding firm. Anybody over there asks you about it, you can tell 'em. No sale."

Pete said, "Yes, sir. I'll do that. You have a good day."

The man nodded to us and went back to his work. We crossed the narrow strip of grass between the end of Pacific St. and the sidewalk, and headed back up 16th Street toward the crosswalk.

I said, "There are a few apartment buildings here. Want to bet that Bluefire owns them?"

Pete looked troubled. "I know what the property people on the board need Judge Ostrander for."

"What?"

"Eminent domain."

I sucked in a breath. "They can seize the property if the owners won't sell?"

"The government has the right to take private property for public use. They have to compensate the owners fairly, but if the owners won't voluntarily sell, the county can force the sale."

"*Shit.*"

"Exactly. I hope Sheila can find a link between the board members and Bluefire."

I said, "I have faith in Sheila. If there's a connection, she'll find it."

When we got home Pete went to work in the kitchen, doing his prep for the week. I got out my laptop and went to the website for the county property assessor.

First I checked the addresses of the empty houses we'd seen. They were, indeed, owned by Bluefire. I typed in a few random addresses from the three streets. Over half were owned by Bluefire. Then I checked the apartment buildings. All of them were owned by Bluefire.

I said, "Hey, Pete, suppose one of those apartments we saw might be where the athletes live?"

"Could be. The kid did say they were across the street from the college."

"If so, Bluefire owns them. If one of the board members is behind Bluefire, and the college is paying Bluefire for athlete housing - there's a fat conflict of interest, too."

"Racking them up, aren't we?"

I returned to my search, going to one of the real estate websites to see what was for sale in the neighborhood we'd visited. I noted the addresses, then went to Google to map them - and found something fascinating.

"Pete? Why would the houses just west of 14th Street only be worth two-thirds of those east of 14th?"

"What?"

I carried the laptop to the kitchen. "Look at Bay, Grant and Pacific. West of 14th, the prices range from one to two million. East of 14th, the prices run from $1.5 million to $3 million."

Pete frowned at the screen. "Huh. You'd expect the houses closer to the ocean to be a little *more* expensive, if anything."

"Yeah, you would. And see that?" I pointed at an abbreviated row of five houses on the north side of Bay Street, between the college and the YWCA. "Two of these are for sale, and they're in the same price range as the houses west of 14th. They're priced considerably lower than the houses right across the street from them. Want to bet that those five lots aren't included in the college's scheme?"

"Okay - I must be thickheaded after all the interviews today. Why would the value be higher?"

"If Bluefire sells them to the college, whoever owns Bluefire is going to make a shitload more money than they would if the values matched the neighborhood. And if someone on the board is behind Bluefire..."

Pete whistled softly. "And if Elaine learned something about that... But don't the values come from the county assessor's office?"

"Not sale prices, no. Market value is different from assessed value, although they're related." I went back to the assessor's site and checked their values for the properties that Bluefire owned. "Everything that Bluefire owns is assessed significantly higher than the properties they haven't bought yet."

Pete said, "So. Bluefire offers the homeowners a price slightly over market value, then - what? Does some sort of improvement that gets assessed way too high? Then when the college comes along to buy the property, they have to pay the higher price?"

I picked up my phone. "I'm calling Kevin."

I had some difficulty explaining what I'd discovered to Kevin. He said, "Hang on. Let me open Google Maps... Give me those addresses and numbers again?"

I read them to him. He said, "Holy shit, I see what you mean. So if Elaine learned about this scheme..."

"Then she might have blackmailed someone into reinstating her. Assuming one of the board is behind Bluefire."

Kevin said, "Okay, but why reinstate her? Why not just kill her then?"

"You're asking me? Figure it out, Detective."

He sighed wearily. "Working on it."

Monday, March 27

When I got to the office I dealt with email then began going through the books on my shelves, deciding if I needed any of them for my sabbatical. I'd just chosen a few when my phone dinged with a text message.

It was from Pete. *Got Arizona State. Three classes. Two intro, one abnormal.*

Yay!!! What did they say?

Not much. Have to go to class myself right now.

Dinner out this evening to celebrate?

Sure. Will call you this afternoon.

At noon Liz, Kristen and I met Sheila at our customary table at the North Campus Student Center. Sheila said, "I've been emailing Kevin all morning."

I said, "You found useful stuff?"

"Yes. I wasn't getting anywhere, searching for a human presence behind any of those shell companies. But then I found a teeny, tiny news item - just a line, really - from the business section of the *Times*, back in 1998. It said that Santocean had bought three oceanfront lots in Santa Monica. Guess what stands on those lots now?"

I said, "Harold Hendricks's hotels?"

"That's it. Once the demolition had been done on the decrepit motels occupying the lots, Santocean sold the properties to Hardhat, who made some improvements to the lots then turned around and re-sold them to Quad H Inc."

Liz said, "Quad H?"

I said, "Harold Hendricks Hotel Holdings?"

Sheila said, "Say *that* three times fast, eh? Quad H is Hendricks's company. That one's not a secret."

I said, "So Hendricks and Skipper have done business before."

"Oh, yes. And both profited handsomely from it. *And* - Dawson, Duncan and Hill were the attorneys that drew up all the contracts for those transactions."

I asked, "Was it Sierra Barrientos that handled the deals?"

"No. It was George Duncan, one of the senior partners. But that was eighteen years ago."

Kristen said, "So who owns Santocean?"

Sheila shook her head. "Still searching for that. I suspect it's Harold Hendricks himself, but I can't verify that yet."

I finished my pasta salad and snapped the lid back on the container. "Okay. Let me think out loud here. Suppose that Harold Hendricks is Santocean. In that case, he - through Bluefire - has a financial interest in the properties along 16th Street. The prices are jacked up on them, so he's going to sell them to the college directly, not pass them through Skipper's company first. So how will Skipper make any money from this deal?"

Kristen said, "Skipper's company is Hardhat, right?"

Sheila said, "Right."

"If Hardhat is a development company, Skipper may be aiming for the contract to improve the property. To do the demolition and prepare the property for the college to use."

I said, "But that's a major conflict of interest. Augusta Skipper is the chair of the board - she's going to profit from any contract that Hardhat gets."

Sheila said, "I'd be willing to bet that Augusta's name doesn't appear on any of Hardhat's records, and that her personal finances are completely separate from her husband's business. On paper, anyway. Or maybe Mr. Skipper has his own shell company for circumstances like this."

Kristen said, "And - you've got a lawyer, and a sympathetic judge to manage any disputes."

I said, "The college probably has to get a fixed number of bids for any project requiring an outside contractor. All Augusta has to do is tell hubby what the other bids are, and he can sneak in at the deadline with a bid that undercuts the others."

Liz said, "Maybe Hardhat won't be involved this time. If these people are longtime business associates, this won't be the last opportunity they have to collaborate on a deal."

We sat for a moment, digesting it all. Then Liz said, "I still don't see how this explains Elaine's death."

I said, "She knew of Bluefire. She *must* have known something damaging. If she knew that Hendricks was behind Bluefire - that in itself would be sufficient. If she exposed that, Hendricks would have to either dump the properties or resign from the board. He's not going to let the properties go. And if he resigns from the board, the Real Estate Gang doesn't have a majority anymore."

Kristen said, "The challenge will be to prove all of this."

I sighed. "Yeah."

Pete called at three, just as Liz and I were coming off the reference desk. I said, "Hey, are you home?"

"Yeah, getting some work done so I don't have to this evening."

"What did Arizona State say?"

"That I was the best-qualified candidate, and also the only one who wasn't going to be working a full-time job in addition to being an adjunct, or teaching ten other adjunct classes elsewhere. They liked it that my entire focus would be on their students."

"Did they ask why you were leaving SMC?"

"They did that in the interview. I told them I'd been considering it for a while, that thanks to my spouse I no longer had to work full-time, and some turmoil in our department cemented the decision. Oh - another thing they liked? I was the only candidate who allowed them to call my current employer. The others either didn't have a current employer, because they were adjuncts for hire, or they didn't want their full-time employer to know they were moonlighting."

"I'm sure Elliott and Dr. Canaday gave you strong recommendations."

"Yeah, they told me they did. Arizona State called them Friday after my interview."

"Are you *excited?*"

He laughed. "I guess. I'm still so busy here, it hasn't hit me yet that I'm actually leaving. And... I have a shitload of work to do, to create these new classes. Teaching online requires loads more preparation than face to face. I remember, you worked for weeks on converting that historical research methods course, and then they decided not to teach it online."

"*That* was disappointing. Were they able to tell you what textbooks you'll be using?"

"Yes, both of them. Of course neither is the one we use, but I've ordered them both, so I can get started. And - you won't like this."

Uh oh. "What?"

"Each class has 200 students."

I sucked in a breath. "Holy *shit*. Multiple choice self-grading exams, right?"

"As much as possible. Speaking of which, I should get back to work."

"Right, you said you didn't get as much done in the office as you wanted."

"Yeah, I got interrupted. Tell you about that at dinner."

I got home at quarter of six to find Pete on the sofa with his laptop, muttering under his breath. I said, "Didn't get done grading, eh?"

"No. But I'll be able to finish after dinner." He closed the laptop and stood up. "Do you need to change?"

"Nope. Just pee."

He grinned. "I'll take Ammo out for a pee while you're doing that."

Once Ammo and I had relieved ourselves, Pete and I went out the front door. Pete locked the gate behind us. I said, "We're going to continue that habit?"

"Of course. We got out of the habit after the Ashley Bennett case, but we should have continued to do it. It's much safer."

"And it stops people from stealing our vegetables."

He laughed. "See, I hadn't even thought about that. Bonus. Where do you want to eat?"

We ended up at the Santa Monica Seafood Market's café, site of our first-ever date back in 2008. Once we were seated and had ordered I said, "We've talked about your reaction to Elaine's death, but how do you really feel about leaving the college? You haven't said much about it."

He considered it for a minute. "You know, even though we'd discussed it in theoretical terms - now that it's happened, it's happened so *fast* that I haven't had time to think about it. It may not completely sink in until I close the office door for the last time."

"Do you think you'll miss it?"

"I'm sure I'll miss the daily interactions with everyone. Especially Aaron."

"We'll have to make extra effort to spend time with him and Paul afterwards."

He smiled at me. "Thanks for that."

"For what? Aaron and Paul are my friends, too. I'd enjoy seeing them more often."

"I'll tell you what I *won't* miss. Committee work. Department meetings. Academic Senate. And I'll only have three classes, not five. And, I *hope*, the students will be of better quality."

I grinned. "You said you got interrupted today. What happened?"

"Oh. Alice Greeves came by to congratulate me. She'd been talking to Elliott, and he told her about my new job."

"Are she and Elliott publishing something?"

"Yeah, they have a proposal for a paper due next week."

"Did she say anything about Ethicgreen?"

"Just that she couldn't imagine how the company could be related to Elaine's death. She's been a partner - that's what they call the salespeople - for five years, and it's been smooth sailing. No scandals, no financial monkey business, no controversy. As multi-level marketing goes, Ethicgreen is one of the higher rated companies."

The server brought our dinners, and I picked up my fork. "Between what Zane Wong said yesterday and what Alice told you, I'd guess that Kevin and Jon can drop the Ethicgreen angle."

Pete nodded. "They never drop anything completely until the case is solved. But I agree - it'll probably turn out to be irrelevant."

"Sheila uncovered some information today that may start unraveling the tapestry." I glanced around, lowered my voice, and gave Pete the gist of what we'd discussed at lunch.

"You're right. It sounds logical." Pete stabbed a shrimp and squinted at it. "But you're also right that it's gonna be tough to prove."

Tuesday, March 28

On Tuesday morning I had an appointment with my internist, Dr. Egan Weikal, to follow up after my asthma attack. Dr. Weikal had a subspecialty in pulmonary medicine, which made him ideal to serve as my primary care doctor.

I chatted with the nurse as she took my weight, blood pressure and pulse, and ran me through a battery of pulmonary function tests. Then she left me a gown and told me to wait.

While I was waiting, I got a text from Kevin. *Asking for a subpoena for Bluefire, etc. Don't want to spook Hendricks or the others until we get it.*

Good luck. You don't have to get Judge Ostrander to sign, do you?

NO.

Dr. Weikal came in about 20 minutes later. "Jamie, hello. How are you feeling?"

"Back to normal, from a breathing standpoint."

"Good. Let me listen." He rubbed his stethoscope on his palm to warm it, then listened to me breathe. "You're off all the extra medication now, right?"

"Right."

"Getting any exercise?"

"Brisk walking. I can't run yet."

He nodded at my shoulder. "When does that come off?"

"Friday, I hope."

"Where do you walk?"

"Sometimes on the treadmill at the Y, sometimes through my neighborhood."

He frowned. "I'd prefer the treadmill to reduce your exposure to outside pollutants."

I groaned. "I hate being stuck indoors. Aren't there just as many pollutants inside, with people wearing aftershave, and fumes from carpets and paint?"

"There are indoor pollutants, true. When you walk outdoors, where do you go?"

"Up a side street. Off the main drag." I knew I was whining, but I didn't care. "I grew up outdoors. I *hate* being stuck indoors."

"You grew up in a medium-sized city near the ocean, not in a basin that traps every particle of exhaust from seven million cars." He smiled sympathetically. "Are you still hiking?"

"Between the shoulder and the respiratory issues, I haven't hiked for over a month."

"Your shoulder should be stable enough to hike now."

"It is. We're going hiking in the mountains this weekend. Next weekend we go to New Mexico, and we'll do a lot of walking. But I can't go to the mountains every evening."

"No." He sat back and crossed his arms. "The reason I'm concerned is that your PFTs -" pulmonary function tests - "haven't entirely recovered after this episode. They should have. You're very gradually doing damage to your lung tissue. That has to stop."

That was a shock. "But I feel *fine*."

"Your peak flow is within normal limits, so you wouldn't sense shortness of breath, but it's only recovered to 95% of your predicted level. It should be 100% by now." He rubbed his chin. "You've been exercising in the evenings?"

"Yes. After dinner."

"Switch to mornings. The morning air is cleaner since there's been less traffic overnight."

"Okay."

I must have sounded as dejected as I felt. He said, "Don't be discouraged. Over time, your lungs should repair themselves - but you've got to give them the chance. That means lowering your exposure to irritants. When are you moving to New Mexico?"

"Um - we don't know yet. Probably not for two or three years."

Dr. Weikal frowned. "That's unfortunate."

I said, "We are spending two months in the UK and one month in Alamogordo this summer. We'll be away from LA for nearly three months total."

"Glad to hear it. You've got your coworkers trained not to wear scent, right?"

"Oh, yes, but sometimes a student will come through with something on."

"Sure, that'll happen. We're not going to hide you in a bubble." He tapped his forehead. "But avoiding your asthma triggers has to be at the forefront of your mind, *all* the time. When are you leaving for the UK?"

"June 26."

"Three months. Make an appointment to see me before you go." He scrawled on the front sheet of my chart and handed it to me. "I don't want to see you *before* then."

Meaning in the emergency room. "Me either."

He shook my hand and left. I made my appointment, and trudged to the library.

There wasn't much traffic in the center of campus; it was mostly contained on the outer edges. Maybe we could come here and walk Ammo in the evenings. That would mean driving, though - I'd always thought it ridiculous to drive somewhere just to walk.

That attitude might have to be modified.

I'd emailed Abby the blueprints for our house the day after I'd spoken with her. We'd invited her to dinner this evening, to go over the plans and talk about what we wanted built in the house. Pete and I were going to Alamogordo weekend after next, and we wanted to give Mitch, our builder, a heads up.

Abby arrived right on time. I introduced her to Ammo, and she spent several minutes rubbing his belly, which naturally endeared her to him for life. Pete was completing meal preparations, so I pointed Abby to the sofa. "Have a seat."

"Thanks. What did you do to your shoulder?"

I explained. "Two more days in this thing."

"Ugh. You did that before, right?"

"Right." I didn't add, *right before we got the inheritance.* That would stir up issues that I didn't want to discuss, and knew Abby didn't either. "So your business has exploded, eh?"

"Yes. I still can't believe it sometimes." She smiled. "After I sold the house I contacted Kevin, tried to transfer the money to him, but he wouldn't accept it."

"*Oh.* I didn't know that."

She shrugged. "We texted back and forth about it over a day or so, and that was it. Anyway, once I had that chunk of money, I was able to pay my brother-in-law's friend who's a web designer to do a website for me, and I was able to buy a higher quality saw and stock up on some other supplies. I made business cards and started handing them out to everyone I came in contact with. You'll never *guess* who my first major order was from."

"Someone I know?"

"Yep. Martie Pepper."

Martie Thrash/Pepper, would-be actress and owner of the Gravity Channel, formerly the Conspiracy Network. "You are *shitting* me."

She laughed delightedly. "You know, they kept us on board to build the sets for that new show, *The Quantum Gene?* We spent enough time on set that Martie and I got to know each other a little bit. When she found out I built furniture, she hired me to do her entire dining room. She wanted a farmhouse atmosphere."

Abby's specialty was Shaker-style furniture. "That's fantastic."

"Yeah. She not only paid me a bundle, but she told all her friends and neighbors. Orders started flying in. We'd wrapped up the first season of *The Quantum Gene*, so it was the ideal time to tell Eddie I was quitting." She spread her hands in a "voila" motion. "That was almost five months ago. It used to take me a week to complete an order, because I only had one or two at a time. Now it's a month."

I said, "Abs, that is terrific. I'm so pleased it's worked out for you."

She smiled, almost shyly. "Thank you. As it turned out, it was thanks to the inheritance. If I'd had to split the money from the sale of the house with Kevin, I wouldn't have been able to get started as soon."

"You didn't spend it all on the website, did you?"

"God, no. That only took about a tenth of it. I used some of it to upgrade my equipment and some to buy materials before I started getting paid. I don't require a down payment, so I had to lay out some money for wood before I started building. But I still have half of the house money."

I grinned. "Speaking of houses…"

"Yes. I can't wait to go over the specs with you."

Pete leaned down over the counter. "You'll have to wait a while longer. Dinner's ready."

We didn't rush through dinner. Pete had made baked ziti, a dish that he knew Abby liked. We told her about the geothermal and solar infrastructure for the house, which interested her. After dinner Pete loaded the dishwasher, and we gathered in the living room with the house plans.

Pete spread the blueprints on the ottoman so we could all see them easily. I pointed to the room that would be our office. "This is the office, and we'd like to have built-ins on these two walls, similar to what you did upstairs."

"Sure. You're not going to share a desk?"

Pete and I said in unison, "Oh, *hell*, no."

Abby laughed. "I bet Jamie's too much of a neat freak for you, Pete."

Abby, Kevin and I had shared an apartment for four years. She knew me well. Pete said, "I have to spread out to work. He doesn't like it when my papers infringe on his space."

I said, "Which will not be a problem in the new office. It's large enough that we can each have our own desk and shelving. We have plenty of spare bedrooms, so we don't need a sofa bed in the office."

I said, "We'd like you to build the desks, too, so they match the cabinets. Unadorned tables, like the one upstairs."

"Sure. What's your flooring going to be?"

Pete said, "Bamboo in the bedrooms and office, tile everywhere else."

"Okay. Should we earthquake-proof these cabinets?"

Abby had created all the cabinets in our current office with doors and drawers that would remain closed in an earthquake, and had gone to extra effort to firmly attach the structure to the wall. Pete said, "The risk is much lower in Alamogordo than it is here. But it couldn't hurt to drive extra anchors."

"Okay." Abby had brought a legal pad with her; she wrote *Office* and made several notes underneath it. "What's next?"

After Abby left we cleaned up the kitchen together. Pete asked, "Did you hear from Kevin today?"

"No. I wonder -" I stopped as my phone beeped with a text message. I looked at the screen and began to laugh.

Pete asked, "Kevin?"

"No. Avery Roth."

Pete and I had met Avery at a California Library Association conference in Oakland, over two years previously. She was a librarian at Stone Canyon College, another of LA's community colleges. She'd aided Liz and me in figuring out who'd killed her library director, and we'd remained friends.

Pete said, "No kidding. What does she want?"

"For me to call her." I hit dial.

She answered immediately. "Jamie Brodie! Still stumbling across the occasional dead body?"

I laughed. "A few, here and there. How *are* you?"

"I am well. I wanted to pick your brain."

"About what?"

"UCLA's history department. I got accepted to the graduate program for fall."

"No *kidding!* That's fantastic. I'll be your librarian!"

"I know, right? But I'm supposed to contact one of the professors in my field of interest, with the intention of eventually doing research with that person, and I need a recommendation on who to contact."

"Ah. What's your field of interest?"

"The *best* field, obviously. Ancient history."

I laughed. "You and I are going to be *best* friends, Avery."

"I know. But - I'm interested in Rome. The only ancient history faculty listed are specialists in Jewish, Greek and Byzantine history. I don't know which one to ask."

"Ah. I'd go with Reuben Wolfe. He's the Jewish history specialist. Ancient Jewish history and Roman history are all tangled up with each other."

"Okay. Do you know him?"

"I know him well. You want an introduction?"

"*Yes!* Please!"

I chuckled. "I'll email him this evening."

"Oh my God, thank you. You're my new best friend. I want to stop by the library sometime next week. You can give me the grand tour."

"You bet. Text me first so I'll be free."

"Of course. See you soon."

I sent an email to Dr. Wolfe in the history department, telling him about Avery, then followed Pete upstairs. "I just received another reason to stick around YRL for another couple of years." I told him what Avery had said.

He laughed. "Oh, Lord, the trouble you two can get up to… Does that make you feel better about your job?"

I grinned. "It sure does."

Wednesday, March 29

The next morning when I got to work I had a return email from Reuben Wolfe. *Jamie, thank you for your information about Avery. I remember reviewing her application; she sounds like a wonderful addition to the department. I'd be delighted to meet her in person when she's on campus. Please bring her by.*

I texted Avery - *Dr. Wolfe very positive about you, wants to meet when you're here next week* - then got to work.

My morning was scheduled with back to back research instruction sessions in introductory classes. It was exhausting to teach more than two classes in a day, but I preferred to group them together and get them over with as soon as possible. I taught from 9:00 straight through until just before 1:00, giving myself five minutes to gulp down my sandwich and meet Liz at the reference desk.

I told her about Avery, which delighted her. "That is *fabulous.* We'll have so much fun. But she has to quit her job - how is she going to afford a doctorate?"

"I didn't ask her about finances. Maybe she's been scrimping and saving."

"Maybe she's going to live with her parents."

Clinton appeared before us, smiling. "The word of the day is *imposture.*" He bowed and headed for the stairs.

Liz said, "Imposture? Is that poor posture?"

I found the definition. "No. It's pretending to be another person. What an imposter does."

Liz screwed up her face quizzically. "Who do we know that's pretending to be someone else?"

"I expect Clinton is referring to our shell companies. I'm anxious for Sheila to dig out their secrets."

I was on the bus when Pete texted me. *Just leaving the office. Falafel House?*

Sure. See you shortly.

When I got to our front gate I squinted into the distance and could see Pete on the far side of Arizona Avenue. I waved but he didn't respond. I went into the house, leashed Ammo, and took him out the front gate, locking it behind me.

Pete spotted us as he was crossing Arizona and brightened, picking up his pace. We traded packages - the bag of food for Ammo and his poop bag. Ammo found a suitable spot on the strip of grass between the street and sidewalk and commenced pooping. I said, "What kept you late at work?"

He glanced around and lowered his voice. "Another visit from the board."

"Seriously? All of them?"

"No. Skipper, Hendricks and Barrientos." He bent down to pick up Ammo's mess.

"What did they want?"

He straightened back up and tied a knot in the plastic bag. "They were with another guy. I believe he was an architect."

"Were any of them lurking in your office this time?"

"Not mine. They spooked Audra, though. She came back from the bathroom and found them there." He made a sour face. "They just walked into my office and started talking about the renovations as if I wasn't there."

We went in; Pete dropped the poop bag outside the back door while I set the food on the table. We both washed our hands and sat down. I said, "I guess they know who's leaving. They didn't suppose it was worth talking to you."

He shook his head. "Still pretty damn rude, though."

When we'd eaten, Pete wadded up our dinner debris and tossed it into the kitchen garbage can. "Want to go for a walk?"

"*Yes.*" Pollutants be damned.

We changed from our work clothes, leashed Ammo, and followed our normal route up Arizona. Pete said, "What time is your orthopedic appointment on Friday?"

"At 8:45."

"And you'll get out of your contraption?"

"Assuming I pass the stability tests, which I should. I've been 100% compliant."

"Yes, you have." Pete patted me on my much-battered shoulder. "You're a model patient."

"Thank you."

"If you want to do some practical physical therapy, on Sunday we could go to my office and start cleaning it out. We'll drive so we can load the car up. If we do that two or three times over the rest of the term, I should be able to close the door and walk away come June."

"Sure. I don't know how much I'll be able to lift." My shoulder and upper arm muscles had noticeably - at least, I noticed it - lost mass.

"I'll carry books. You can go through papers."

We walked quietly for a minute, savoring the cool air. I said, "How do you really believe you'll like teaching online?"

"I'm not sure." Pete twisted his mouth. "Not as much as face to face. I expect this is going to be temporary, to keep me busy until I figure out exactly what it is that I want to do."

"Maybe being a campus counselor?"

"Maybe." He grinned. "Maybe NMSU-Alamogordo will have a position available one of these days."

Thursday, March 30

As I was passing the circulation desk the next morning, I stopped to congratulate Andy. "How's the wedding planning?"

He chuckled. "From what I can tell, progress is being made. Jessie's doing most of the…"

Andy paused when a student approached carrying a book. I backed away so it wouldn't seem like he was busy. He smiled at the girl. "Hi, can I help you?"

The girl thumped the book - *An Atlas of Ancient Greece* - onto the counter. "There's something wrong with this book."

Andy's smile turned quizzical. "Wrong how?"

"The table of contents and index don't match what's actually in the book." She turned to the table of contents and pointed. "This is supposed to have a detailed map of Thessaly. But…" She turned to a page in the book. "It's not here. The book is misprinted. See? The numbered plates go from 33 to 35. There's no 34."

Andy flipped the pages back and forth. "You're right. Maybe it appears at another location in the book?"

"No, I looked. It's not there. I *really* have to locate that map."

A suspicion sparked in my brain, and I moved back toward Andy and the student. "May I see?"

The girl shoved the book toward me. I laid it flat on the counter and pushed the pages apart as possible at the spine of the book - and saw that my suspicion was confirmed. "It's not a misprint. Look at this."

There was a tiny stub of Plate 34 left, so thin that it wouldn't be noticed with the atlas open normally. The plate had been cleanly sliced out of the book.

Andy said, "*Crap.* Someone *cut* it out?"

I said, "Apparently."

The student gasped. "People *do* that?"

I said, "Not very often, fortunately. Is this map for a particular assignment?"

"Yes. We were supposed to…" She trailed off as a thought seemed to strike her. "I bet it was John David."

Andy asked, "Who's John David?"

"He's an *asshole* in my class. This is the sort of thing he'd do, just so the rest of us couldn't complete the assignment."

I said, "Do you know John David's last name?"

"Bailey. John David Bailey."

"Who's your instructor?"

"Dr. Wolfe. History of Ancient Greece."

"Okay." I picked up the atlas. "Let's find you another map of Thessaly, then I'll speak to Dr. Wolfe."

I accompanied the student back to the atlas section and found an appropriate map for her to consult, then carried the damaged atlas back downstairs. Before going to the history department, I stuck my head in Gerry O'Brien's office.

Gerry was our geography librarian. He and I had a mutual loathing society and avoided each other assiduously. But if other atlases had been messed with, he might know.

He was at his computer, surrounded by books and papers. He glanced up at me and scowled. "What the hell do you want?"

"Nice to see you too, Gerry." I laid the atlas on his desk and pointed out the damage. "Has anyone mentioned cut pages from atlases to you?"

"No." He leaned forward and ran his finger down the cut edge. "This was done with *precision*. Who would do that?"

"The student who reported it suspects another student." I closed the atlas. "It's a history class. I'll handle it."

"Yeah, do that." He turned back to his monitor.

I couldn't help myself. "Always a pleasure to talk to you, Ger. See ya later."

He snarled. I smirked and headed for Bunche Hall.

Reuben Wolfe - Avery Roth's soon-to-be adviser - and I had a great relationship, and had co-authored a paper a few years ago. He was also at his desk, surrounded by books and papers, but was much more welcoming. "Jamie, hello! How are you?"

"Hey, Reuben, I'm fine." I nodded at the stack. "What are you working on?"

"A paper on Masada. George Morgan has been doing some research for me."

"I bet he's loving that." George was our archaeology librarian. "I won't hold you up, but I have a question. This was reported by one of your Ancient Greece students." I showed him the cut page.

Reuben frowned and, like Gerry, drew his finger down the cut edge. "That's *terrible*. Does this happen often?"

"Fortunately, no. But the student suggested that it might be one of her classmates. John David Bailey. What's your opinion of that hypothesis?"

Reuben shook his head. "Bailey's a worm, but he wouldn't have been this careful. Are you familiar with the Forbes Smiley case?"

"The map thief? Yes." Forbes Smiley was a map dealer who'd been convicted of stealing rare maps from several major universities. He'd removed them from books with an X-Acto knife. "Damn, might we have a Smiley at work?"

"It's possible. Although I'm not sure that particular map is extremely rare."

"It's not, because this atlas was in circulation, not Special Collections." I closed the book. "If not money, what would the motive be?"

"Perhaps someone is decorating his or her apartment." Reuben smiled. "Good luck."

As I headed back to YRL, I had an idea - and texted Avery. *Can you come to campus today, by any chance?*

If it's this afternoon, yes. What's up?

We require a spy.

Oooh, oooh! Whatever it is, I'm in. I'll be there around 2:00.

Cool. Come to reference.

See you then.

Avery arrived at reference at 1:45, nearly squirming with excitement. "I'm all set to go undercover! See?"

She was dressed in black from head to toe. Liz and I both laughed. I said, "Your hair is not exactly inconspicuous."

Avery slapped her hand to her hair, dyed the color of a green parakeet. "Oh. Should I wear a hat?"

"No, no. You just need to pass for a student." I explained. "Hang out at a desk on the fourth floor and watch for anyone cutting pages out of atlases."

"Cool. What if I see someone?"

"Text me."

"Excellent!" She jumped to attention and snapped a salute. "Private Roth on duty, sir!"

Liz and I both laughed. I said, "Give yourself a promotion. You can be a corporal."

She grinned and headed for the staircase.

A few minutes after Avery left, I got a text from Kevin. *YOU ARE NOT GOING TO FUCKING BELIEVE THIS.*

What????

Preliminary DNA on hairs from Elaine's bedroom. Got a partial hit in CODIS.

Partial?

50% match. Hairs belong to the son of someone in the system.

Who??

BELINDA MARCUS.

I sucked in a breath. *HOLY SHIT. Josh Marcus and Elaine??*

Apparently. OMG.

Liz said, "What? What?"

I said, "Hold on," and typed to Kevin, *How would they have met??*

My screen started flashing with an IM from Sheila Meadows before I could read Kevin's response. Sheila had typed, *Got the names behind companies, and found out for sure that Lithian was buying the properties for Bluefire.*

I texted Kevin, *Wait a sec - IM with Sheila. She has names.* To Sheila I typed, *Yes! Who?*

Santocean is Harold Hendricks. Lithian is a front for JBM Holdings, which is wholly owned by a guy in Marina del Rey named Joshua Marcus.

I froze, staring at the screen. Liz said, "What *is* it?? You look like you've seen a ghost."

"I have. Hang on." I texted Kevin. *Santocean is Harold Hendricks. Lithian owned by JBM Holdings in Marina del Rey. JBM is Josh Marcus.*

OMFG.

Now what?

Now we question him. HFS.

Can I be there?

You bet. You're off tomorrow for Cesar Chavez, right?

Right. Dr. appt for my shoulder at 8:45 am.

We'll schedule Josh for 10:30. Will let you know if that changes.

Liz was practically hopping up and down. "What? *What?*"

"Remember Belinda Marcus? Found guilty for hiring the killers of Gavin Barkley and Alexandra Crabtree?" Gavin Barkley was the drunk driver who'd killed my mom. Belinda, one of my mom's best friends, had been in the back seat and was rendered quadriplegic in the accident.

"Sure, I remember. You and your dad had to testify."

"Did Jon or I tell you about her son? Josh?"

"Yeah. You all thought he was involved too, but his mother wouldn't implicate him."

"Right." I pointed to my screen. "Josh Marcus lived in Marina del Rey. Sheila found that one of the companies behind the land deal at SMC is in Marina del Rey. Owned by a guy named Joshua Marcus."

Liz gasped. "Oh my *God.* How many Josh Marcuses could there be in Marina del Rey?"

"Only one. *And* you won't believe *this.*" I told her about the DNA.

Liz lowered her voice. "Holy *fuck.* Is he doing something illegal?"

"I don't know. It's definitely unethical. If he's paying off an appraiser to artificially inflate the values of those properties - that must be fraud."

Liz grabbed my forearm. "It's gonna be like OJ. He got away with murder, but they gave him a long sentence for theft. Your Josh won't get away with this." She pointed at my monitor. "See if you can find him online."

I searched for *Josh Marcus Marina del Rey* and found a LinkedIn profile. I clicked on it, and Josh's smug face smirked out at me. *CEO of JBM Holdings.*

I said, "There he is."

Liz asked, "Why would he create a shell company if he wasn't doing anything illegal?"

I couldn't answer that.

At about 2:30 Pete texted me. *Home now. Talked to Kevin. Did he tell you about Josh Marcus?*

YES. Interview is arranged for 10:30 tomorrow. Should be fascinating.

I can't wait.

Just before 4:00, I got a text from Avery. *Bogey sighted. Big guy. Bring reinforcements.*

Hm. I sent an IM to Frank Villareal, the only other male librarian on staff who could handle himself in a fight. *You busy? I need some extra muscle for a few minutes.*

To do what??

To catch a thief.

On my way.

Frank had been Army Special Forces. I figured that between the two of us, we could manage any "big guy."

Of course, said big guy was armed with some sort of knife. I sent another IM, this one to Demetrius Garmon in Special Collections. Demetrius was 6'5" and built like Dwayne Johnson.

The guy with the knife couldn't take out all three of us.

When Frank and Demetrius arrived a moment later I told them what we were facing. We concocted a strategy and took the elevator to the fourth floor. Once there we fanned out. Demetrius went to the end of the H stacks, Frank flanked around the Fs, and I cut through the middle right to the G section, where the doctoral student desks were located.

Avery spotted me, and nodded to a figure standing at the G stacks. I turned, saw who it was, and stopped. "Oh, for God's sake."

Stephen Atcheson slapped the book that he was examining closed. Frank approached behind me and said, "*Stephen.* Why am I not surprised?"

Stephen looked back and forth between us frantically. He was struggling to be cool, but it was impossible. "What? Why are you here?"

From behind Stephen, Demetrius said, "Atcheson. You stealing from the library?"

Stephen whirled around. "Huh? *Stealing? Of course* not."

Frank said, "Let's take a gander at that briefcase, shall we?"

There was a battered briefcase at Stephen's feet. Demetrius picked it up and produced two maps. "Well, how about that?"

I dug my phone out of my pocket and called 911.

After work we held an impromptu celebration. Kevin and Jon were still on duty, but Avery, Liz, Lance, Justin, Andy, Jessie, Pete, and I all gathered at Kristen and Kevin's condo for pizza and beer. Liz lifted her bottle for a toast. "Here's to the sight of Stephen being led away in handcuffs. I shall treasure it always."

Everyone said, "Hear, hear," and we drank. I said, "And here's to Avery, sleuth extraordinaire, who saved the YRL map collection."

The others cheered. Avery graciously accepted the accolades. "Thank you. Thank you very much. I couldn't have done it without backup."

Justin said, "He was *selling* them? He couldn't have been making much money."

Faced with a police interrogation, Stephen had admitted everything. Antonio Jenkins, the arresting officer, had called me with the details afterward. I said, "He wasn't. Reuben Wolfe was right, the maps were being used as wall art. Stephen was selling them online for about $30 each. Plus shipping."

Jessie asked, "What will happen to him?"

Pete said, "Petty theft is a misdemeanor. The maximum sentence is a year in county jail, but he may only get probation, assuming this is his first offense. He'll probably also have to reimburse the university for the value of the books he damaged."

Liz said, "He'll have trouble finding a job. He won't have the money to pay restitution."

Kristen said, "He'll have to sell a couple of his precious Dean Koontz first editions. What a *shame*."

We all drank to that. Lance sighed contentedly. "Work is going to be *so* delightful now."

I said, "You all will be shorthanded for a while."

Lance and Andy looked at each other and grinned. Andy said, "We don't *care*."

On the way home I was still chuckling about Stephen's stupidity. Pete gave me an indulgent smile. "I know you're thrilled to see him go."

"Thrilled and *relieved*. Like you would be with Elaine, if she hadn't been reinstated and had stayed alive."

"Yeah. It's always preferable to have a problem solved without anyone dying."

"Mm. Apparently, someone at SMC couldn't dream up another method to solve the problem of Elaine."

Pete shook his head. "Josh Marcus."

"I know, right? Un-fuckin'-believable."

"Yeah." Pete guided the car into our parking space and cut the engine. "Let's hope he knows who killed her."

"Assuming he didn't do it himself."

Friday, March 31

Pete was also off for the Cesar Chavez holiday. He drove me to the doctor's office, then took Ammo for a walk across campus. I was jealous.

After the nurse called me back, I waited about fifteen minutes for Dr. Eniwaye, my orthopedic surgeon. He came in smiling. "How's the shoulder?"

"You tell me. I've been very compliant."

He laughed. "I'm sure you have been. Have you had any discomfort?"

"No, but I haven't done much with it."

"Okay, let's see what we're dealing with." He stood in front of me and had me move my shoulder in several different directions, which hurt - as I'd known it would. Then he had me push against his hand in several different directions, which also hurt.

I sighed. "Ow."

"Don't worry. You're right where you should be. Shall I send you to physical therapy?"

"No. *Please* don't. I still have all the exercise sheets from last time."

"And you'll be just as compliant with them as you have been with the restraint?"

"Yes, *sir.*"

He grinned. "Okay. See you in six weeks."

I'd arranged to meet Pete at the intramural fields. I walked toward them letting my arm dangle, gingerly swinging it at the shoulder just a centimeter or two. It felt unstable, although I knew it wasn't.

I swore to myself that I'd never do this again.

Just like I'd promised myself two years ago, at the same stage in my recovery.

I sighed. In a little over six weeks I'd turn 37. My lung function was below par, my left arm was connected to my body by ever-loosening threads...

I was getting old.

We took Ammo home then power-walked to the police station, getting there at 10:15. The duty officer handed us our visitors' badges and buzzed us through. We found Kevin and Jon at their desks. I asked Kevin, "Does Josh know you're on this case yet?"

"No. Elias and Tim went to visit him yesterday. Josh won't see me until I walk into the interview room." Kevin nodded at my restraint-free shoulder. "Everything okay?"

"Yeah. Now I get to do six weeks of therapy, but I can do it at home."

Jon said, "It's almost time. Let's get you two situated."

Pete and I took our all too familiar seats in the observation room and waited. Five minutes later the door to the interview room opened. Elias Pinter guided Josh in and said, "Make yourself comfortable, Mr. Marcus. Can I get you anything?"

"No, thanks."

"All right. I'll be back." Elias left.

Pete said, "So that's Josh Marcus."

"Yup."

I hadn't seen Josh since the trial, a year ago. He'd gained some weight, and his face was puffy. Pete said, "He's a drinker."

"How can you tell?"

"Years of observation."

"He's gained weight since last year."

Pete nodded. "Drinking would be a logical response to his mother's guilty verdict."

"Pfft. I doubt that he's capable of experiencing guilt."

Another five minutes passed. Josh glanced our way a couple of times. He appeared to be suppressing the urge to fidget. I figured he knew he was being watched by *someone*.

Jon entered the room first, Kevin right behind. The expression on Josh's face when he saw Kevin was priceless. Dismayed shock. Shocked dismay. Blended with a soupçon of fear.

Kevin sat down right across from Josh. Jon took the other seat and said, "Mr. Marcus. Fancy meeting you here."

Kevin gave Josh what could only be described as an evil grin. "Hiya, Josh."

Josh gulped. "Ah - Kevin. Good to see you again."

Kevin's grin widened. "Oh, it's my pleasure. How's your mom?"

Belinda had been sentenced to house arrest for life, without parole. Josh looked like he wanted to throw up. "She's - ah - as well as can be expected."

"Glad to hear it." Kevin crossed his arms and kicked back a little bit. "So, Josh. You're in some hot water."

"Hot water? What are you talking about?"

"Lithian Properties."

Josh blinked a couple of times. "Uh - Lithian?"

"Yup. Are you gonna tell me you've never heard of it?"

I saw Josh consider, then choose the right answer. "No."

"No, you've never heard of it?"

"No, I'm not going to tell you that." Josh squirmed. "Lithian is a subsidiary of my company."

"Uh huh. Tell me about this subsidiary."

Josh gulped. "Ah - um - I buy and sell properties. There are times when it's beneficial for my name to - ah - not appear in the paperwork. Lithian allows me - ah - a degree of anonymity that's sometimes necessary."

"In what circumstances would that be necessary?"

Josh waved his hands around a little bit, eyes darting around the room. "The circumstances are all different. It's hard to give an example."

Kevin glanced at Jon and they both grinned - which made Josh start chewing on a thumbnail. Kevin said, "We'll come back to that. Tell me about Bluefire Company."

Until that moment, Josh hadn't realized why he was being questioned. Now he had. He turned as white as Wonder Bread. He practically squeaked, "Bluefire?"

"Yup. Bluefire."

"Ah - Bluefire is - um - an investment I made."

"An investment."

"Yes. It - er - provided me with some extra capital. A way to expand the business, you might say."

"Tell me how that works."

Josh cleared his throat. "There are two companies within Bluefire. We pursue separate projects, but we pool a percentage of our profit. That way we have extra cash on hand to get a project started, without having to involve a bank."

"There are two property companies?

"Yes."

"What's the other one called?"

"Um - Santocean Limited."

"Uh huh. Who's the man behind the curtain for Santocean?"

"His name is Harold Hendricks."

"Do you and he do business together?"

"No. We don't. Bluefire is - it's like I said. It's just a financial vehicle."

"But either of you can use Bluefire to create deals."

"Right."

Kevin said, "Did you or Hendricks buy the property along 16th Street in Santa Monica? Under the cover of Bluefire?"

Would he admit it? Josh cleared his throat. "Er - I did."

"Who advised you to do that?"

"No one."

"No? You just thought you'd get into the rental business in Santa Monica on a whim?"

Josh gritted his teeth. "Santa Monica College is surrounded. It can only expand outward. I thought the college might someday be interested in buying the property on the other side of 16th Street. If the college never wanted it, at least I'd have solid income from renters."

"And you thought of that all by yourself."

"Yes." Josh was rigid.

I said, "He's lying, right?"

Pete said, "Yes."

Kevin asked Josh, "Harold Hendricks had nothing to do with the 16th Street property?"

Josh leaned forward and spoke pointedly. "No. He did *not*."

Pete said, "Huh. Now *that* rings true."

I said, "Harold will indirectly gain from its sale, though."

Kevin asked, "If it wasn't Harold, who was it?"

"I *told* you. I found the property myself."

Kevin and Jon glanced at each other again, but they didn't grin this time. Josh decided to take offense. "I'm not stupid, you know."

Kevin turned his gaze back to Josh, and Josh shrank back in his chair. Kevin said evenly, "Maybe not. Tell us about Elaine Pareja."

Josh blinked at the sudden turn in questioning. "*Oh*. Uh - Elaine and I dated for a while. We broke up months ago."

"How did you meet?"

Josh licked his lips. "We were introduced by a mutual acquaintance."

Kevin raised an eyebrow. "Name?"

He sagged a little. "Harold Hendricks."

I said, *Bam*. Harold lied when he said he didn't know Elaine's boyfriend."

Kevin asked Josh, "When did Harold introduce you?"

"It was at a fundraiser at one of his hotels. We all sat at the same table."

"How did you and Elaine get along?"

"Fine."

"Why did you break up?"

Josh's face darkened. "I found out she was fucking one of her *students*."

"Bet that pissed you off."

"Of course it did." Josh caught on. "Wait. Whoa, whoa, whoa. I did *not* kill Elaine."

Kevin said, "Convince me. And don't use your mother as an alibi."

Josh ground his teeth but didn't acknowledge that remark. "That was two weeks ago, right? I was in Hawaii. I got back last week. I have my boarding passes at home, and the phone number of my hotel."

"We'll need those."

"You will have them."

"Any idea who might have killed Elaine?"

"No." But Josh's expression was furtive.

I said, "He's lying about that?"

Pete studied Josh through the window. "I don't believe he knows. But he suspects someone."

"Who do you know on the Santa Monica College Board of Trustees?"

Josh was sweating, and blinked again at the change in course. "Only Harold."

Kevin said, "Are you sure about that?"

Josh tried to laugh. It didn't work. "Why would I know anyone else on the SMC board?"

"You'll be doing business with them, won't you? If they ever decide to buy that land you own?"

Josh's eyes were darting around the room again. "Sure, but who knows if or when that will ever happen?"

This time it was Jon who sighed. Kevin said, "Josh." He tapped on the table in front of Josh. "This is important. Pay attention."

"I *am*."

"We are going to arrest you for felony intent to defraud the State of California. If you tell us who tipped you off about buying the 16th Street property, we'll consider amending the charge to a misdemeanor."

I didn't think Josh could turn any paler. But when Kevin said *arrest*, Josh's face lost any semblance of color. "*Fraud?* I haven't *committed* fraud!"

"No, you've committed *intent* to defraud." Kevin smiled. "It's an easy records search to find out who your favorite appraiser is. I know from experience that you don't care about saving anyone's skin but your own. I'm willing to bet that appraiser will tell us everything about *you* in return for leniency. But you can help that all go away. We won't even call your appraiser if you tell us who pointed you toward 16th Street."

Josh gulped, his eyes wild. "I told you. I found the property myself."

"Okie dokie." Kevin pushed his chair back. "Detective Eckhoff, care to do the honors?"

"My pleasure." Jon stood up. "Joshua Marcus, you are under arrest for intent to defraud the State of California. You have the right to remain silent…"

Pete said, "Whoever set Josh up to buy the property? He's more afraid of that person than he is of going to jail."

"But you believed him when you said that wasn't Hendricks."

"Yeah." Pete frowned. "I could be wrong."

"I was considering that it might be Elaine - but he admitted his involvement with her, and she's not around to be afraid of."

"No."

In the interview room, Jon read the Miranda statement. Josh said, "I want to call my lawyer."

"By all means." Jon handcuffed Josh's hands in front of him. "We'll do that right now."

Kevin said, "Josh?"

Josh was sullen now. I'd seen that face before, in court. "What?"

Kevin grinned. "You tell your mom I said hello."

Josh turned red but wisely bit back whatever it was he wanted to say. Jon said, "Right this way, Mr. Marcus."

Pete and Kevin spent several minutes discussing Pete's reactions to Josh's statements. Jon enlisted Elias to accompany him to Pacific Division to book Josh - West LA didn't have a jail of their own. I said to Kevin, "He won't be in jail long, will he?"

"Probably not. I expect his attorney will meet them at Pacific and get the ball rolling. They should be able to find a judge to set bail by this evening."

Pete said, "Hendricks lied to you. About several things."

"Yup. When Jon gets back, we're going to pay him a visit."

Pete and I walked home. I retrieved the moist heating pad from the linen closet where I'd stashed it two years ago, and the sheet of shoulder exercises from my file of medical information. Pete microwaved a wet towel for me, and I sat with the towel and heating pad on my shoulder for twenty minutes. At that point I removed the heat and Pete supervised my exercises, very gently assisting me to stretch just beyond where I wanted to stop. He asked, "How long will you do therapy?"

"Last time I didn't get my full range of motion back until I was able to swim again. That's six extra weeks." I wiggled around a bit, getting comfortable. "I promised myself that I'll never do this again."

Pete gave me a *yeah, right* look. "Are you going to play rugby again?"

"Um - that's the idea."

"Then you'll dislocate your shoulder again."

"Gee, thanks."

He shrugged. "You will. In college, we had a right fielder on the baseball team whose shoulder popped out every time he stretched for a fly ball. He'd lay on his back and pop it in again."

"Ack. This is only my third time."

"I know. You'll do it again."

"I'm going to do my best not to."

"I know, but you won't be able to stop yourself, any more than my teammate was able to stop himself stretching for fly balls." He slapped my knee and stood up.

It was a lovely evening, so Pete decided to grill. He was just lifting the chicken breasts out of the marinade when the doorbell rang. I said, "I'll go."

It was Jon and Kevin. I unlocked the gate and escorted them to the back deck. "Did you see Hendricks?"

Jon said, "Yep. Found him in his office. He folded like a card table."

I asked, "Did he admit everything?"

Kevin said, "Not everything. He admitted knowing Josh, owning Santocean, and introducing Josh and Elaine. He admitted the deal that he made with Bob Skipper and Sierra's law firm, using Santocean, to build his hotels - but that was before any of them were on the SMC board. He denies that he was the one who told Josh about the 16th Street idea, and he denies having anything to do with Elaine's death."

Pete said, "Do you believe him?"

Kevin made a face. "Not entirely. He's still squirrely."

Jon said, "So we have hatched a *scheme*."

I said, "Uh oh."

Kevin grinned. "Pete, the next board meeting is this coming Tuesday, right?"

"Right. First Tuesday in April."

"We're going to ask Celine Bachmann and Zane Wong to perform a little theater for us. If they agree, we'll get Celine to talk about the owners who won't sell, and what sort of obstacles that will cause. It should be a fascinating discussion. Then we'll get Zane to ask if anyone else finds it curious that all this land stuff wasn't uncovered until Elaine died."

Pete grinned. "I'd like to have a ringside seat for that."

Jon grinned back. "We'd expect nothing less."

The next morning Pete and I packed up Ammo and his supplies and headed for Topanga Canyon to meet Kevin and Kristen. They'd beaten us there, and were waiting at the trailhead for us. Ammo enthusiastically greeted both of them. I said, "Jon and Liz aren't coming?"

Kevin said, "No. Jon has to go to the range to qualify."

Kristen said, "And Liz was going shopping with Jessie for wedding dresses."

Pete asked Kevin, "Is Jon a good shot?"

"Above average. Not as good as me."

I laughed. "No one's as good as you."

Kevin tried to be humble, and failed. "True."

We set out, climbing steadily. I tried to breathe deeply, encouraging my lungs to expand. Kevin asked, "How's your shoulder holding up?"

"Hm? Oh, it's fine. I was concentrating on my breathing."

Pete stopped. "Are you short of breath?"

"No, no, no. I'm breathing in plenty of clean air."

"Okay." Pete began walking again. "Should you be swinging your arm or something?"

"Probably." I tried, gingerly. I didn't have much range of motion, but something was better than nothing. "I decided yesterday that I'm getting old."

Kristen, who had turned forty the previous year, laughed. "We're all getting old, kid."

We were alone on the trail - it was still early - but Pete still glanced around before he asked Kevin, "Did you guys get your subpoena yet?"

"No. The DA wouldn't sign off. Said there wasn't adequate cause. We're meeting with Celine Bachmann and Zane Wong this afternoon to sketch out our approach for Tuesday night. The public is welcome at the meetings, right?"

"Right." Pete gave Kevin a sideways glance. "You're hoping that Hendricks or someone else will be shaken up enough to say something incriminating?"

"That's the idea. You guys will both meet us there?"

I said, "I didn't sit through all those interviews to miss out on the ending."

Back at the parking lot - back in range of cell towers - Kevin's voicemail tone sounded. He listened to the message then said, "That was Brian Marcus, returning my call. Mind if I call him back?"

Kristen said, "Go ahead."

Kevin placed the call. "Hi, Mr. Marcus. I'm well, thanks. Yes, I'm afraid it's about Josh. I wanted to ask you a couple of questions."

Brian must have agreed. Kevin said, "What do you know about Josh's businesses? Is he successful?"

I could hear Brian's derisive laughter through the phone. Kevin gave me a knowing smirk. "I guess that's a *no*. Three bankruptcies? Jeez. Okay, let me explain what he's done."

Kevin gave Brian an outline of the 16th Street situation. "Would Josh have had the idea to buy up that property by himself? I didn't think so either, but I wanted to confirm. Oh? Who did you think it was?"

Kevin listened for a moment. "Yes, her name was Elaine. Did you ever meet her? I see. No, no. Josh has a firm alibi for the time of her death. We're just untangling all of the business relationships. Have you ever heard the name Harold Hendricks? No? Okay."

I whispered, "Ask about Belinda."

Kevin gave me a thumbs up. "Thanks, Mr. Marcus. I appreciate your help. How is Belinda?"

He listened for a moment, shaking his head slowly. "I'm sorry to hear that. Yes, sir. Will you stay in Oceanside? Ah. I'm sure your daughter would love to have you close by. You know, you should call my dad. He'd be delighted to hear from you. Okay. Thanks again. Bye."

Kevin hung up. "Brian believes that Elaine told Josh about the 16th Street property. Would she have done that?"

Pete shook his head. "We only began hearing about the new student center a couple of months ago. Josh was buying up property long before that. It doesn't strike me as something that Elaine would concern herself with."

I said, "That does strengthen your impression that it wasn't Josh's idea."

Kevin nodded. "If someone on the board clued him in - maybe that's what Elaine found out."

Pete said skeptically, "Would that be worth killing her for?"

Kevin said, "Sure, if she was threatening to throw a monkey wrench in the works. We're talking about a shitload of money. Josh has spent most of old man Barkley's money on these properties."

I said, "Seems like the person with the most to lose would have been Josh, though."

"True, but Harold Hendricks would also profit, since he's half-owner of Bluefire."

Pete held up a finger. "And don't forget the Skippers. Even if their company wasn't involved, either Bob or Augusta could have decided that Elaine was too much of a threat to their business associates."

I said, "Or maybe Josh hired out his dirty work again."

Kevin scowled. "Yeah. We know he's capable of it."

I asked, "How is Belinda?"

"Not well. She got the flu over the winter, which turned into pneumonia, and she hasn't completely recovered. Brian thinks she wants to die."

I said, "Her purpose in life was to see Gavin Barkley dead. She has nothing left to live for."

Pete and I arrived at Kristen's Bel Air home at 7:00, bearing the game Clue Classic which I'd wrapped in a page from the Sunday comics. Kristen had provided a couple of sandwich rings, chips and dip, and a cake. We added our gift to the stack and filled our plates. The ladies were in a clump, apparently discussing Jessie and Liz's dress-shopping expedition. Pete and I sat with Lance Scudieri and Justin Como, whom Pete hadn't seen since Lance and Justin's own wedding in November, a week and a half after the presidential election. James Wygant, our access services director, was with them.

I said, referring to Stephen Atcheson, "So, James, your life just got considerably simpler."

"No kidding." James waved a section of sandwich at me. "Do you know what the cops told me? *Why* Stephen was stealing maps?"

I said, "For extra money, I guess?"

"Yes, but the *reason* he needed extra money was that he'd met a woman with expensive tastes and he wanted to impress her."

Justin and I exchanged an amused glance. Lance asked, "Is this the woman he met at speed dating?"

James nearly choked on a bite of sandwich. "*Speed* dating? Atcheson went to speed dating? Where?"

I said, "At a queer club in Venice. My friends Ali and Mel saw him."

"A… Did Atcheson know this?"

Lance said, "Not when he got there."

"So who is this woman he ended up with?"

I said, "We don't know. But she had to be either bi, trans or a drag queen."

James stared at us for a second then laughed uproariously. "That's the best news I've had in *years*."

Sunday, April 2

On Sunday morning we went for an early run. I tried to swing my left arm as normally as possible; it was easier to do with my elbow bent, but still wasn't comfortable by any means. When we got home I applied the moist heat again, then did my exercises, then repeated the heat treatment. Pete and I showered, leashed Ammo, and drove to SMC with several empty cardboard boxes in the cargo space.

I said, "It'll be okay for Ammo to be in the building?"

"Sure. He'll be fine."

"I know *he'll* be fine. I don't want anyone else freaking out when they see a dog in the building."

"I doubt there will *be* anyone else in the building."

We parked right by the entrance - easy to get a spot on the weekend - and climbed the stairs to the psychology department. Pete unlocked the outer door to the office suites then locked it again behind him.

No one was around. Every office door was closed. Pete unlocked his and left the door ajar. He set down the boxes he was carrying; I instructed Ammo to lay in the corner.

Pete laid his phone on his desk, then propped his hands on his hips and scanned the office. "Okay. You have the file cabinet. Toss anything over a year old or SMC-specific. Anything that's left, I'll go through."

"Okie dokie." I removed a handful of files from the top drawer and pulled up a chair.

Pete went out in the hallway and returned with a paper recycling bin, which he set beside me. I said, "What if I find something with personal information?"

"You won't. That's all at home."

"Can we have some music?"

"Sure." Pete turned on his computer and went to his Mumford and Sons station on Pandora, lowering the volume so that only we could hear it. Ammo stood up, circled three times, and lay back down with a sigh.

We'd brought six boxes, as many as the cargo space would hold with Ammo also in the car. Pete reserved five of them for books, allowing me one for papers. As I sorted, I realized that I probably wouldn't fill an entire box. Most of what I was finding was meeting minutes and copies of older journal articles. I was likely to create an overflow in the paper recycling bin.

We'd been working for about an hour when Ammo lifted his head. He didn't stand, but he began making his rumbly pre-growl noise. Pete and I looked at each other; Pete cut the sound on the speakers. A few seconds later we heard the outer door to the office suite being unlocked.

Ammo stood up, now fully growling. I said softly, "Ammo, sit."

He sat, but he kept growling. I said, "Ammo, quiet."

A few seconds later we heard the door next to Pete's being unlocked. I gave Pete a "who?" look; he mouthed, "Audra" to me. The door didn't close; we could hear someone, maybe Audra, moving around in the office.

I'd about decided that nothing else would happen when Audra appeared in the doorway. "Hi, Pete! I saw the light from your office in the hallway. I didn't realize you'd be here."

Pete said, "Hi, Audra. You remember Jamie?"

"Sure." She smiled at me. "From Aaron's wedding. It's good to see you again."

"You too."

Ammo had stopped growling, but he was still on alert. Audra said, "Wow. What an *impressive* dog."

Pete said, "This is Ammo."

Audra laughed lightly. "Ammo. That's an ideal name for an ex-policeman's dog." She nodded to the boxes. "I guess you're starting to clear out, too."

"Yep. Figured I might as well get started on it."

"Exactly." Audra beamed. "I heard late Friday from Glendale Community College. I start there August 15."

Pete said, "Hey, that's super! And closer to home, right?"

"Yes. Anyway - I thought if I tackled the office a little bit at a time, it wouldn't seem like such a massive undertaking." She smiled. "I should let you get back to it."

Pete said, "Let me know if you need anything."

"Sure." She turned away. A second later we heard her open a file cabinet drawer.

We worked for another hour, by which time Pete's book boxes were full. He sorted through the papers I'd not thrown out, and tossed most of them. I said, "You've got another empty box now."

"Yeah." Pete picked up a box of books and carried it into the hallway. "I'll leave that box here. I haven't cleaned out my desk drawers yet. I'll start on that this week, and I can use that box for the things I'm going to keep."

"Should we go to the library from here?"

Most of Pete's books were geriatric editions that he wanted to donate to the public library. "Yeah. We can grab lunch on the way home."

"I can't lift a box of books yet."

"No, no. I'll carry them. You just handle Ammo."

Pete carried the boxes to the car one by one. When he came back for the last one, I leashed Ammo and walked him out as Pete locked his office door behind him. He stuck his head in Audra's office. "You gonna be okay by yourself here, Audra?"

"Sure." She pushed a loose strand of hair from her face. "I'm nearly done myself. Just lock the outside door."

"Will do. See you tomorrow."

"Yep." Audra smiled and turned back to her file cabinet.

We were barely through the office suite door when Audra yelped then called, "Pete?"

Pete dropped the box and darted back inside. "What?"

I followed at a slower pace, being forced to overcome Ammo's reluctance to reverse course. When I got back to Audra's door, she and Pete were staring into her bottom file drawer. I said, "What is it?"

"It's a pair of bloody gloves." Pete took out his phone.

Audra's eyes were wide. "Who the hell would have left those there?"

Pete said into the phone, "Hey. We're at my office and Audra Rock is here too. She just found a pair of blood-stained gloves in her file cabinet drawer. Okay." He hung up. "Police are on their way. Audra, when was the last time you were in that drawer?"

"Several weeks ago. Those Mardi Gras beads are the last thing I threw in there."

I leaned in for a glimpse. The gloves were resting on a tangled knot of beads. I said, "But the police searched everyone's offices after Elaine's death, right?"

Pete said, "Right. A week ago Monday. They weren't there then."

Audra had recovered from her shock and was getting mad. "The only other people who have been in here are those *board* members. And now the cops will suspect *me* again. *Damn* it. When will they know if they're the right gloves?"

"It'll take a few days. The GSR test is quick, but it'll take longer to send the blood for DNA and try to lift prints from the gloves."

It took Kevin and Jon about a half hour to arrive, but they brought SID techs with them. Many photos were snapped of the gloves in place, then Kevin donned his own gloves and lifted them out of the drawer. He let the SID photographer snap a couple of pictures, then passed them to a second SID guy, who dropped them into an evidence envelope.

Audra was pale. "Am I in trouble?"

Kevin said, "Not if we can find out who these belong to."

Audra said firmly, "Why would I be so stupid as to hide them in my own office?"

Kevin smiled. "I don't believe you would."

She blew out a breath. "Well. Thank you for that, I guess."

Jon said, "Dr. Rock, let's step out in the hallway. You can tell me about the board's visit to your office."

SID didn't stay long. They found fingerprints on Audra's filing cabinet, which I figured had to be Audra's own. Whoever hid the gloves surely wouldn't be dumb enough to leave prints on the drawer handle.

Of course, there was still the possibility that Audra had dumped them there herself. Although I found that unlikely.

SID packed up and left. Pete escorted Audra to her car, while Kevin, Jon and I stood in the hallway to confer. Jon said, "Audra claims that the only people who have been in her office since last Monday, other than everyone else in the department, are Hendricks, Skipper and Barrientos."

Kevin said, "That doesn't rule out Curtis Glover."

Pete walked back in, heard what Kevin said, and grimaced. Jon said, "No. But if we can't tie the gloves to him - or Audra - there's nothing else to go on there."

I said, "It's got to be one of those three."

Kevin said, "Or, if more than one person was involved, the shooter could have delivered the gloves to one of the board members to dispose of."

Pete said, "Augusta named Audra as the person in our department who vouched for Elaine. It would make sense if Augusta dumped the gloves on Audra."

Jon said, "Hendricks has the most to lose financially. He's the only one that's already involved with the land deal."

I said, "Other than Josh."

Kevin said, "Right. But we know Josh didn't kill Elaine."

Jon said, "But if it wasn't Hendricks or Elaine who told Josh about the land in the first place…"

Kevin threw up his hands. "I don't know. Let's hope our one-act play on Tuesday evening rattles Skipper or Hendricks to the extent that one or both of them does something stupid."

Monday, April 3

Monday was the first day of class for spring quarter. I'd get busy later in the week with classes and research requests, but for a couple of days the library would be quiet. I decided to celebrate the first day of the quarter and the month of April by treating myself to a frappuccino. Now that I could run, I could burn off extra calories.

Clinton's word of the day was *ultracrepidarian*. I said, "Wow. That's a doozy."

Liz looked it up. "It means 'giving opinions beyond one's area of expertise.' That's what we do every time we answer a reference question that's out of our specialty."

I said, "Not exactly. Our answers aren't opinions, they're educated advice."

Liz snickered. "Speaking of being out of our specialty - Jon said you and Pete had a three-year plan."

"It might be a two-year plan - but probably three. We'll see. We're moving to Alamogordo at *some* point."

"What will you do there?"

I shook my head. "Beats the hell out of me. They have a community college. I suppose they might need an adjunct instructor."

She wrinkled her nose. "Community college students? You'd *hate* that. You don't even like *our* undergraduates."

"It would only be part-time. Maybe one class. I can't just waste all this education."

She gave me a sideways look. "You'd be wasted in a community college."

"Not necessarily."

She snorted. "Yeah. You would."

That evening I told Pete what Liz had said. "You know community college students. Do you think I could work with them?"

"Do I think you could work with them? Yes. Do I think you'd excel at it? Yes. Do I think you'd enjoy it? Not a *chance*."

I groaned. "Then what am I gonna do? I can't *wait* to move into our new house. I *have* to get out of Los Angeles for the sake of my lungs. But I have to have something to *do*."

"I'm not worried. We'll come up with something. If we can produce food to the extent I have in mind, that's going to require a lot of input from both of us."

"I'm not exactly *worried*. The topic continues to pop into my head, though."

He grinned. "Maybe the book you're going to write this summer will be an international bestseller. You can become a full-time writer. You could be the Doris Kearns Goodwin of Scotland."

I had to laugh. "What's going on at the college?"

"Not much. Did you talk to Kevin today?"

"No. Did you?"

"Yeah, late this afternoon. He's searching Audra's background to see if she has any connection with the board members. Forensics confirmed that there was GSR on the gloves. DNA will take longer, but the blood type was consistent with Elaine's. They also think they can get DNA from the skin cells shed inside the gloves by the wearer."

"I still don't get it. If someone on the board killed Elaine, why would they stow the gloves in Audra's office? Looks like they'd prefer that they were never found."

"I don't know. But remember, Augusta Skipper gave Audra's name as recommending Elaine's reinstatement. If Augusta killed Elaine, she might have decided to point the cops in Audra's direction by planting the gloves."

"Maybe Audra lied about not knowing anyone on the board."

Pete sighed. "Maybe she did."

Tuesday, April 4

The next morning, I drove to work. I'd just left the parking structure when I got a text from Pete. *I asked Audra about board connections. She said she didn't have any.*

How would Augusta Skipper know her name to offer up to Kev and Jon, then?

Dunno. May have just scanned the website and picked the only remaining female.

The SMC board meeting began at 4:00. I left work after reference at 3:00, picked up Pete at home and drove to campus.

The board met in a conference room in the administration building, at a circular table in the center with extremely cushy seating. Another, larger circular table surrounded the inner one, effectively separating the board members from whomever else might be in the room.

I was surprised to see that there were quite a few other people in the room - including one man with a videorecorder on a tripod. I nudged Pete. "The board has these meetings filmed?"

"No. That guy is known to everyone on campus. He's a conspiracy theorist. He hangs out at the library all the time, searching for evidence of governmental wrongdoing. He runs for a seat on the board every election and never gets more than about a hundred votes."

"Is he a student?"

"No. Just a concerned citizen."

"Bizarre."

"Yes. But useful, in this case. Jon and Kevin will be able to ask him for a copy of the recording."

I looked around the room. "Who are all these other people?"

"Um - some of them are department chairs, some of them are from the administration. The guy over there in the checked shirt is the Academic Senate president. The guy next to him in the suit is the college president. Some of the others are from different constituent groups within the college."

I glanced at my watch. "Kev and Jon are about to be late."

I'd no sooner spoken than the two of them walked through the door. The room was settling down, but when Kevin and Jon stopped a few feet inside the door and did a slow survey of the room, silence fell like an anvil.

I watched the faces of the board members. Augusta Skipper was staring. William Ostrander seemed wary. Charles Mullins leaned over and said something to Celine Bachmann; Celine shrugged and made an "I don't know" face. Zane Wong cocked his head to the side in interest, pretending he didn't know what was going on.

Harold Hendricks was attempting to appear nonchalant, but he'd gone white as a sheet.

And, I noticed for the first time, Sierra Barrientos wasn't there. That shouldn't be a complication, though. If our theory was right and either Harold or Augusta was the killer - or *knew* who was - her presence or absence wouldn't make any difference.

Everyone else in the room was staring, mostly out of curiosity. Kevin and Jon had their game faces on - Kevin's, impassive and intimidating; Jon's, a just-swallowed-the-canary smirk that said, "I know something *you* don't."

The guy with the camera had swung it toward the door. Jon gave the camera a scant nod, and he and Kevin came to their seats. The guy pointed the camera back at the board.

Augusta regained her senses and picked up a gavel, thumping it on a circular slice of wood. "Meeting is called to order. First item: roll call. Celine Bachmann?"

Celine said, "Here."

"Sierra Barrientos texted me five minutes ago. She's behind a wreck on the 405. Harold Hendricks?"

Hendricks's face was still pale, and he'd been flicking glances toward Kevin and Jon ever since they arrived. He said, "Here."

"Charles Mullins?"

"Here."

"Bill Ostrander?"

"Here."

"Zane Wong?"

"Here."

"All right. Are there any public comments?"

There weren't. Augusta moved through approval of minutes briskly. There were no guest speakers. Augusta said, "All right. Old business. Celine?"

Showtime.

"Thank you, Augusta." Celine passed around handouts.

Kevin leaned over to me. "Those are copies of the 16th Street maps."

Celine said, "Now that the state has allocated funds for the property along 16th Street, I thought it was time to initiate an investigation into some of the details. We've been discussing the property as a block, when in reality, it's owned by several different entities. In particular, there are six homeowners - I've indicated the locations of the homes on the map in front of you - who own their houses outright and have refused other offers *several* times. As you can see, those houses are positioned such that the student services complex as it's currently proposed cannot be built. This is going to present a dilemma, and I propose that we start a discussion on how to approach it."

Harold Hendricks said, "Well, Celine, one thing I've learned through *experience* is that every property owner has their price. We may have to pay a premium, but I'm sure those lots are obtainable."

"That's the thing - I'm not sure they are." Celine was playing her role flawlessly. "I spoke to one homeowner in particular, who said he'd been offered twice the appraised value of his home by a company that wants to turn it into a rental, as many of the other homes in that neighborhood already have been. He has an invalid wife who doesn't want to abandon her home of fifty-plus years. We're not just dealing with property, we're dealing with human lives here."

Augusta said snarkily, "Of *course*, Celine, we're aware of that."

Celine sighed. "I'm just *saying*, this could shine a negative light on the college. The word is out in the community, obviously, that we intend to build on that property. I learned about the people who won't sell when I took a drive around that neighborhood. All six of them have enormous signs in their yards that say, 'Not for Sale at Any Price.' The news outlets will eat this up."

Judge Ostrander said, "I expect the public will be equally sympathetic to the requirements of our students. There are far more of them than six. It might be a challenge to garner much sympathy for a handful of stubborn geriatrics who are trying to gouge the college and the taxpayers."

Celine held up a finger. "That's another thing. Let's talk about gouging the college and taxpayers." She passed out a second sheet of paper.

Kevin leaned over to me again. "Google Maps overlaid with the information you gave me."

Celine said, "Look at this. The houses between 14th and 16th are priced at least fifty percent higher than those between 14th and Euclid. It's the same neighborhood. The houses further west are closer to the beach. If anything, they should be worth more, but they're not. Something smells fishy here."

Charles Mullins said, "You mentioned a company that's been buying homes in that area to turn into rentals. Is that who's jacking the price up? Who is this company?"

Celine said, "I checked the property assessor's website. All of those homes were bought at ten to fifteen percent above market value by a company called Bluefire Holdings. Now this Bluefire wants to turn around and sell to us at *fifty* percent above market value?"

There was murmuring among the spectators. Zane Wong said, "Who owns this Bluefire company? It sounds like we should have a discussion with them."

Harold Hendricks opened his mouth to speak, and Kevin and Jon's gazes went to him like laser beams. It threw Harold for a moment. "I'd - ah - indeed. But I'd expect that when Bluefire bought the properties, they did improvements, then had another appraisal done. There's not much we can do about that."

Harold wasn't admitting to the board that he owned half of Bluefire. Of course, if we were right, Augusta - and maybe Bill Ostrander - already knew that. Zane said incredulously, "Improvements for a rental that are worth $500,000? What, did they install solid gold toilets?"

Augusta said primly, "There's no need for sarcasm."

Charles Mullins said, "No, but there is need for an investigation on our part. Celine, can we find out who's behind Bluefire?"

"We can. I know someone at UCLA's business library. They should be able to tell me."

Zane said, "I move that we assign Celine to do the background on Bluefire Holdings, as a portion of our due diligence in acquiring the property."

Charles said, "Second."

Augusta was gritting her teeth. "Motion made and seconded that we task Celine with discovery into Bluefire Holdings. Discussion?"

Harold said weakly, "I don't think this is necessary."

Charles said, "Why not? If there *is* something unsavory going on, we can't afford to expose the college to it. Better to find out now."

Celine said, "The college has made plenty of unsavory news lately, with the reinstatement and subsequent *murder* of that psychology professor. As you know, that investigation is *far* from over, and the college is obviously still under scrutiny."

Zane said, "We have to get out in front of this Bluefire business. We don't want any further stupid mistakes, like when we reinstated that woman."

I was enjoying the hell out of this, and I figured Pete was too. Harold opened his mouth again, then closed it. Augusta snarled. "Further discussion?"

No one said anything. Augusta said, "All right. All in favor of the motion as stated, say 'aye.'"

Celine, Charles, Zane - and, astoundingly, Bill Ostrander - said, "Aye."

Harold looked like he was going to throw up. Augusta was sending hateful glances to Ostrander, but said, "Opposed?"

Harold said, "Nay."

"The motion passes. Celine, you'll have a report for us at our next meeting?"

"Yes."

"All right. Any further discussion on the topic of the 16th Street property before we move on?"

Zane said, "I do have one question."

I held my breath. To my right, Kevin leaned forward slightly.

And then, to my astonishment, Harold Hendricks said, "So do I. We've been talking about this property deal for months now. Does anyone else find it odd that we never heard anything about this Bluefire business until after Elaine Pareja was murdered?"

A murmur ran through the room. Kevin didn't move. Jon leaned forward, resting his forearms on his knees, watching Hendricks with interest. Hendricks, for his part, was shooting virtual death rays into Augusta Skipper.

I whispered to Pete, "Hendricks suspects that Augusta killed Elaine."

"Mm hm."

Augusta said tartly, "Harold, you're out of order. Zane has the floor."

Zane relaxed. "As it turns out, that was my question exactly. I find that *decidedly* odd."

Celine said, "Now that you mention it - Harold, what's on your mind?"

Hendricks crossed his arms. He was still staring at Augusta. "From what Celine says, this Bluefire entity is somewhat - mysterious. What if Elaine was involved in it, somehow?"

Augusta was glaring back at Hendricks. Bill Ostrander said, "That's crazy. How would a psychology professor be connected to a property holding company?"

Zane said, "Why not? Elaine was a businesswoman. She was a sales partner in my company and made more money from that than she did as an instructor. Maybe she had other business interests as well."

Augusta thumped the gavel on the coaster again. "We're veering into speculation. Let's leave the solving of Ms. Pareja's death to the police. Moving on."

Hendricks dropped the subject, but he and Augusta stared daggers at each other throughout the entire meeting. The board rapidly dispensed with the rest of their business and heard from the Academic Senate president and a couple of students about various topics. Augusta adjourned the meeting.

The spectators began to scatter. Hendricks cornered Augusta, but backed off when he saw Jon approaching. I said to Kevin, "Now what?"

Kevin sighed. "Now we invite Mr. Hendricks to the station for an interview."

Jon was speaking to Hendricks. I saw him smile widely and say something, then he came back to us. "Mr. Hendricks will meet us at the station in thirty minutes. For what good it'll do us."

Pete said, "He wants to implicate Augusta."

Kevin said, "Hendricks either believes Augusta did it, or he wants us to believe it. But, I don't think Hendricks would have tried to draw the connection between Elaine and Bluefire - potentially exposing his involvement with Bluefire - if he'd had anything to do with Elaine's death."

The room emptied. Celine and Zane nodded to us as they left; Augusta scurried past without glancing at us. The conspiracy theorist with the camera was packing up. We walked outside - only to find Taylor Vinson hanging out at the door. When he saw Kevin and Jon he was taken aback. "Dude. I don't have anything on me."

Jon said, "Why are you here?"

"I wanted to catch my mom. I wanna borrow her car tomorrow."

Pete and I moved away. Kevin said, "Your mom wasn't here. She got held up behind a wreck on the 405 and never made it to the meeting."

Taylor was puzzled. "What would she be doing on the 405?"

Jon said, "She wouldn't come that way?"

"No. She refuses to drive on the 405. If it's her driving, she always goes another way. She had a wreck there herself like ten years ago, and it scared the shit out of her. Besides, she lives on 12th north of Montana and her office is at 3rd and California. Why would she get on the 405?"

Kevin and Jon looked at each other. Jon took out his phone and called someone. "Hey, it's Eckhoff at West LA. Have you had any major incidents on the 405 in the past few hours? Okay, thanks." He hung up and said, "No wrecks on the 405 that stopped traffic since yesterday."

Taylor said, "See? She would have taken some other road." He sneered. "I bet she just wanted to blow off the meeting."

Jon said, "You're probably right."

Taylor moped. "I guess I'll ask my dad instead."

Kevin said, "It's a school night. Don't you have curfew?"

"Yeah..." Taylor checked his watch. "Shit! It's in five minutes." He took off at a run across campus.

Jon made another call. "Elias, you still at the shop? Jill, too? Yeah. Do us a favor before you leave? Go to this address -" He rattled off Sierra's "- and pick up a woman named Sierra Barrientos for questioning. She's a suspect in Elaine Pareja's murder, and she lied about where she was this evening. No, don't arrest her. She's a lawyer, so watch yourselves. Thanks, man." He hung up.

Kevin said, "You guys coming with us?"

I shrugged. Pete said, "Sure."

Harold Hendricks snagged the last visitor parking space at the West LA station. We had to drive three blocks beyond to find a spot. By the time we got back to the station, Harold was parked in an interview room. Pete and I slipped into the observation room as Kevin and Jon began their conversation with Harold.

Jon said, "Mr. Hendricks, thanks for coming in. Who killed Elaine?"

Harold blinked at the suddenness of the question. "I don't know."

"But you suspect Augusta Skipper."

Harold rubbed his forehead, as if banishing a headache. "Yes."

"Why?"

Harold sighed deeply. "When Elaine learned that she wasn't being promoted, she called me, demanding that the board overturn the decision. I said I couldn't arrange that, and she said I'd be sorry if I didn't. I didn't say yes immediately, but told her I was willing to bargain. We arranged to meet at a hotel in Anaheim."

Jon asked, "Why Anaheim?"

"I don't know. That was Elaine's idea. She was paranoid."

"What happened at the hotel?"

"I tried to reason with Elaine. I explained that the board had never interfered in the promotion process, that it would immediately draw suspicion to her, but she was adamant."

"Did she threaten you?"

"Yes. She said that she'd expose my involvement in Bluefire if I didn't cooperate." Harold rubbed his forehead again. "I was an idiot, entangling myself with that Marcus kid, but I didn't have time to do anything about it. I told Elaine that I'd have to convince a majority of the board to go along with it, and she said, 'Then you should get busy.'"

Jon said, "What happened then?"

"I called Augusta the next morning and told her everything. She didn't want to get involved with Elaine's situation, but I was able to convince her. I couldn't sell my interest in Bluefire quickly enough, and if I resigned from the board, Augusta would lose her majority. So she agreed, but she was *deeply* unhappy about it."

"So why do you think that Augusta killed Elaine?"

Harold spread his hands in a helpless gesture. "Who else would have?"

Jon folded his arms across his chest. "Then what happened?"

"The next day we met - the entire board - for our special meeting to ratify the legitimate promotions. After the meeting we presented our decision to the college president, and he said that Elaine had been *fired*."

"Did he tell you why?"

"Yes." Harold closed his eyes and shook his head. "I was appalled, but relieved. There wasn't any point in overturning Elaine's non-promotion if she was terminated."

"Then what happened?"

"Augusta had arranged for the four of us - Bill and Sierra along with Augusta and me - to have dinner after the meeting, to discuss my - er - proposal. On the way to the restaurant, Elaine called me. She said that now she needed to be reinstated. I told her to forget it, that the others would never agree, because she'd been involved with a student. She said I'd better make it happen, or not only would she spill the beans on Bluefire, she'd -" Harold paused. "Well. Elaine was aware of several indiscretions of mine."

Pete made a sound of disgust. "How uncomplicated would the world be if middle-aged men could keep it in their pants?"

Kevin hadn't said a word; he was watching Harold carefully. Jon asked, "What happened at the restaurant?"

"Once we were seated Augusta said to me, 'I presume the reason for this informal meeting is now moot.' I said, 'I'm afraid not,' and told the others everything. Then Augusta and I argued for a while."

"What about Bill and Sierra?"

"Bill said he'd go along with me, on the condition that I sell my interest in Bluefire by July 1. I agreed. Sierra didn't seem to care one way or the other. Augusta gave in. She said she'd wait until morning to send the notice for the emergency meeting, and maybe the other three wouldn't be able to come with such limited notice."

"But Zane Wong showed up."

"Yes. Fortunately, we'd mapped out our approach, in case Zane, Charles or Celine had come to the meeting. Zane didn't know why Elaine had been terminated. He voted against her reinstatement, of course. As it turned out, Augusta could have as well without changing the outcome. But she voted with us." Harold made a wry face. "I've known Augusta for a long time, and I have knowledge of some of her dirty laundry, too. She and I didn't speak of that, but we both knew that I had leverage over her."

I said, "Jeez. What a nest of vipers."

Pete said, "Mm hm."

Jon asked Harold, "Was Augusta or her husband's company involved in the 16th Street property scheme at all?"

"No."

Jon said, "One last question. Besides you, who else does Josh Marcus know on the SMC board?"

Hendricks was surprised. "Well, of course he knows Sierra. She's the one who introduced us."

Jon saw Harold out while Kevin spoke to us. "Sierra's in place in the other interview room. You guys just switch places."

We went to the other observation room and studied Sierra. She didn't appear to be worried - she appeared to be pissed off. Pete and I watched her pace the length of the room several times. When Kevin and Jon entered, she turned on them. "Am I under arrest?"

Kevin said, "Of course not. What would we arrest you for?"

She glared at him. "Then why am I here?"

Kevin gestured to the chair. "Why don't we have a seat?"

She didn't like it, but she sat. Kevin sat across from her and leaned forward. "You're here because you lied to Augusta Skipper about why you missed the board meeting. I find that curious."

Sierra threw her hands out. "I was called out of town for work. It's none of Augusta's business."

"You were called out of town for work?"

"Yes. The partners are sending me to Las Vegas for a couple of days to meet with a prospective client."

Kevin said, "Uh huh." He held up a finger, took out his phone, and made a call. "Hi, Tasha, it's Kevin Brodie."

Tasha Jimenez. Mel's college roommate and law school classmate who was now a partner in Dawson, Duncan and Hill. Pete chuckled.

Kevin was saying, "I'm well, thanks. No, this is police business. Have you or the other partners in your firm asked Sierra Barrientos to go out of town on business this week? No? You don't have a prospective client in Vegas?" He'd been watching Sierra as he spoke; now he smiled. "You're not even members of the Nevada bar. Fascinating. That's yet to be determined, but it's entirely possible. You bet. Thanks, Tasha." He hung up and said, "Tasha Jimenez says there is no client in Vegas. That's two lies, Sierra, and one of them was to me. That was a poor decision, because now I'm *intensely* curious."

A muscle was jumping in Sierra's jaw. If I noticed it, I was sure that Kevin did. She remained silent. I asked Pete, "Why isn't she asking for legal counsel?"

"My guess? She believes she's smart enough to handle this herself. Besides, she's not under arrest."

Kevin leaned farther across the table. "How do you know Josh Marcus?"

Sierra blinked. "Josh Marcus?"

"Yes. Harold said that you introduced him to Josh."

Her eyes narrowed. "He's used our firm for several property transactions over the past four years."

Kevin relaxed and rocked his chair back on two legs. "Let me tell you something about myself, Sierra. I've known Josh Marcus since I was *born*. His mom and mine were close friends. His dad and mine were Marines in the same command at Camp Pendleton. Josh and I grew up together. We had *play dates*."

A slight exaggeration; we'd had one play date that ended disastrously. But Sierra didn't have to know that. Kevin was saying, "Josh Marcus is a sniveling weenie, and he's not very bright. It causes me to wonder why you chose him to buy up the properties along 16th Street. Although I suppose he was a cinch to manipulate."

Two spots of color were forming high on Sierra's cheekbones. She was *mad*. "Josh did *not* tell you that I recommended the property purchase to him."

"No, he didn't. He said he thought of it all by himself. I don't believe that for a second. He did say that it wasn't Harold Hendricks or Elaine Pareja who pointed him toward the properties, and I *do* believe that."

Sierra snorted. "Why?"

"Because I can read Josh like a newspaper. I *know* him. I also know that he'd do *anything* to turn the gaze of law enforcement away from himself. He's got a felony charge hanging over his head. I'm betting that he'll tell us the truth before long."

Sierra was starting to relax. I thought that might be a mistake. She said, "There's nothing criminal in making a recommendation. And I fail to see what this has to do with Elaine Pareja's death."

Kevin thumped the front legs of his chair to the floor. "Did you kill her because Taylor was banging her?"

Sierra stared for a second, then recovered. "Why would I do that? I don't give a rat's ass what that kid does. He's his father's headache."

Pete muttered, "Mommie Dearest. Remind you of anyone?"

I knew he was remembering his own mother. Kevin said, "All righty, then. Here's what I think. Elaine, thanks to her relationship with Josh and her complicated friendship with Harold, knew all about the proposition for 16th Street. Specifically, she knew that you told Josh about the properties to generate more business for your firm. More business for the firm means heftier bonuses for you."

Sierra interrupted. "There's no impropriety there."

"No, if that's where your scheming had ended. But you got greedy. You cooked up a scheme to profit from the sale of the property from Josh to the college. Elaine found out about it. Maybe she was going to blow the whistle, maybe she was going to blackmail you. Either way, she was standing between you and a huge payday. You had to dispose of her."

Sierra was grinding her teeth. She gritted out, "That's absurd. You have no proof."

Kevin smiled and leaned back again. "We found trace evidence - hairs - in Elaine's house that we couldn't match to any of Elaine's known paramours. We also found bloody gloves in Audra Rock's office. We're waiting for the DNA to come back on the hair and the skin cells left inside the gloves. If, as I suspect, the DNA is a 50% match to Taylor, then we have proof." He held up a finger. "And don't forget. I have Josh Marcus."

Jon's phone beeped, and he glanced at the screen. "Josh and his attorney are waiting in the other interview room."

"Fantastic." Kevin grinned. "Ms. Barrientos, you sit tight. We'll be riiiiiight back."

Pete and I trudged back to the first interview room. I said, "We spend so much time in these rooms, we might as well install our own comfortable seating."

"And a fridge. I'm *hungry*."

"Now that you mention it…" I stopped as I caught my first glance of the two men sitting in the interview room. "Well, whaddya know."

Pete followed my gaze. "What? You know Josh's lawyer?"

"I sure do. Gordon Smith, Esquire. Randall Barkley's friend and attorney."

"No shit." Pete studied Smith with interest. "You went to his office to find out how much money you'd inherited from Barkley."

"Yup. That's where we met Drew Jemison. *And* the adult version of Josh."

Kevin and Jon entered the room and took seats, Kevin across from Josh. "Hi, Josh. Mr. Smith."

Gordon Smith inclined his head regally. "Detective Brodie."

No pleasantries, then. Kevin said, "Josh, we've just finished interviewing Harold Hendricks, who told us that you and he were introduced by Sierra Barrientos. Is that true?"

Josh glanced at Smith, who nodded. "Yes. It's true."

"Was it Sierra who told you about the 16th Street property?"

Josh gripped the edge of the table. "Yes."

"How did that come about?"

Josh sighed. "I'd done business with Dawson, Duncan and Hill several times, so I'd known Sierra for a few years. When I found out that I had $38 million coming my way… I was stupid. I called Sierra to tell her that I was looking for a major investment, if she happened to come across any interesting deals. That's when she told me about the college and 16th Street."

I asked Pete, "Why is Smith letting Josh talk?"

"I'm sure he'll jump in if Kevin asks something he doesn't approve of."

Kevin said, "And that's when she introduced you to Hendricks?"

"Yes. She handled the creation of Bluefire, Lithian and Santocean."

"Did you drop the entire $38 million into Lithian?"

"*No*. I kept back $10 million. Sierra wanted me to commit all of it. It made her mad when I didn't. That was the first time I'd seen what was under the classy lawyer facade."

Gordon Smith said, "Ms. Barrientos threatened my client."

"Did she?" Kevin crossed his arms and leaned back. "What happened?"

Josh gulped. "She showed up at my condo. My *home*. She talked her way into the building somehow, and she was standing at my front door. She said that it pissed her off when people didn't take her advice, and if I ever did it again… She knew about my mom. About Gavin Barkley and Alex Crabtree. She said if I ever fucked with her again, that she'd do whatever was necessary to tie me to those murders."

Gordon Smith leaned forward. "Allow me to emphasize that my client had *nothing* to do with his mother's crimes. The only ties that Ms. Barrientos could have disclosed were ones she manufactured herself."

I muttered, "Yeah, right. So why did that scare Josh so much?"

Pete said, "I know Kev's unhappy about it, but there's not much he can do."

Kevin said, "Fine. So, Josh, you told Elaine about all of this?"

"Yes. We talked about the college often because she worked there."

"Naturally. When you heard that she'd been murdered, what did you think?"

Josh blew out a breath. "I couldn't imagine. I thought maybe it had something to do with the students she was involved with. It didn't occur to me that it might involve Lithian or Bluefire. As far as I knew, there wasn't a problem with the property deals."

"Did you stay in contact with Elaine after your split with her?"

"No."

"You didn't know anything about her promotion issues?"

Josh looked confused. "No. Promotion issues?"

"Did Elaine ever say anything or spill any juicy gossip about anyone at the college?"

"No. I mean, she didn't like the other instructors in her department - but if she had any dirt on anyone, she didn't tell me."

"How much did Sierra make when she set up Bluefire and Lithian for you?"

"Harold and I each paid her $100,000."

"Did she bill you every time you bought a house?"

"Yes, plus she'd put herself on retainer." Josh scowled. "She was making a bundle off of Bluefire."

I said to Pete, "So - when it came time to sell the properties to the college, Sierra's name wouldn't appear anywhere, but she'd still profit."

"Yup. And I bet she was doing this on the side, without her firm's knowledge. She's slick."

"Not slick enough."

"No." Pete grinned. "But she might have gotten away with it, if not for her son."

I snickered. "Mommie Dearest gets hers."

In the interview room Kevin said, "All right, Josh, Mr. Smith. The assistant DA is on his way. As soon as he arrives, we'll discuss your future."

Smith said, "My client has been completely cooperative."

"Yes, he has." Kevin stood. "You all sit tight. It won't be long."

We reconvened with Kevin and Jon at their desks. I said, "What now?"

Kevin took a long drink from a bottle of water. "Now we see if Sierra wants to be completely cooperative. I want to wait until we wrap up Josh's case, though. Victor Gutierrez will be here soon."

Jon said, "We can also consult with him about whether we have enough to arrest Sierra."

Pete said, "If you release her, she'll flee."

Kevin said, "Yeah, that's why I'd like to arrest her if at all possible. At least get her in the system."

Jon's phone rang. He glanced at the screen and said, "Ha!" He answered, "Eckhoff."

I whispered to Kevin, "What?"

He held up a finger. Jon said, "Yes, sir. Did you? That is marvelous. What was the name on the receipt?" He grinned broadly.

"Yes, sir, that helps tremendously. Can you email me that receipt?" He rattled off his email address. "Thank *you.* Yes, sir, you enjoy your evening." He hung up.

Pete and I said simultaneously, "*What?*"

"Those gloves we found in Audra Rock's office? The tag inside named the brand, which I recognized. My mother won't wear any other brand. As you can imagine, they're expensive, and not widely sold. I called around, not expecting to get lucky. But I sure did."

I asked, "You found where they were sold?"

"Yup. Only one store carries them locally. It's in Beverly Hills. The manager searched his records, and is emailing me a sales receipt from March 12, when he sold a pair to Sierra Barrientos." His phone beeped; he glanced at the screen and grinned. "And there it is."

Pete said, "Why would she have bought an expensive pair of gloves to kill someone in?"

Kevin said, "Why do rich people do anything?"

Jon said, "I don't know, but I'm glad she did."

On Saturday morning Pete and I went for a run down to the beach then back to Santa Monica College. He'd carried backpacks with him to work yesterday, and we were going to load them this morning with the last of his belongings.

His office already looked bare. The stacks of books and slumping piles of paper were gone. The filing cabinet drawers were nearly empty. There was one shelf of books left.

I said, "Are you going to bring photos home yet?"

"No." Pete picked up one of his framed pictures - a gift from Christine, that portrayed her, Steve and Pete as small children - and smiled. "I'm going to be here eight more weeks. I'll save the photos for my last day."

"Okay. What are we taking today?"

Pete began pulling books from the shelf. "Most of these. I only need to keep my DSM-V and the textbooks."

"Are the textbooks yours?"

"Technically, yes, but I'll leave them behind. Whoever takes over my classes might want them. The department isn't adopting new books until fall 2018. But..." He took down one of the textbooks. "Better make sure I'm not leaving behind any personal notes. Or dollar bills."

I chuckled and began to load the non-textbook tomes into the backpacks. We'd only been working for a few minutes when I heard the outer door to the office suite open.

Verlene Canaday stopped at Pete's door. "Oh, hello! I wondered who could be here - there weren't any other cars outside."

I said, "Hi, Dr. Canaday. We came on foot."

She took in the bare shelves and surfaces. "It looks like you've cleared almost everything out."

Pete said, "Yes, ma'am. We spent a day in here last weekend and accomplished a lot."

I asked, because I didn't know if Pete would. "Will you fill Pete's position?"

"The current plan is that we'll be allowed to fill both Aaron's and Pete's positions. So far, the administration is saying no to

Audra's and Elaine's slots. But Audra wants to adjunct for us, so she'll still teach the developmental psych course." She raised an eyebrow at Pete. "You'd be welcome as an adjunct too, Pete."

He smiled, blushing a little. "Thank you for that. But I'm looking forward to the extra free time and flexibility."

"I don't blame you." Dr. Canaday smiled back. "But if you ever change your mind, call me."

"Yes, ma'am. I will."

I asked, "Have you heard anything about what's happening with the board?"

"Yes. Harold Hendricks resigned yesterday, so there will be a special election next month to fill his and Sierra's positions. The board can operate with five members until July 1, when the new folks will be seated."

Pete said, "Augusta Skipper didn't resign?"

Dr. Canaday snorted. "No. She did step down as chair, and Celine Bachmann was elected by the remaining members to serve out the rest of Augusta's term."

I said, "She should have resigned."

"Yes. But she has stated that she won't stand for re-election next year. So she'll be off the board soon enough."

Pete asked, "I don't suppose they've decided what to do about the 16th Street property yet."

"No. I assume they'll take that up at their next meeting." Dr. Canaday glanced at Pete's wall clock. "I'd better get busy. See you later."

She went to her office. Pete sighed, shaking his head. "I never thought I'd look forward to becoming an adjunct."

"The primary advantage is that you don't have to worry about college politics. Especially as an online adjunct."

Pete returned one textbook to the shelf - not having discovered any money - and removed another. I said, "Will you miss it?"

"You asked me that before."

"I'm asking you again."

He looked around the office slowly, then shook his head. "I'll miss the people. I won't miss this room. Or this building."

"Seven years is a long time."

He smiled at me. "Not in the grand scheme of things."

"True."

"In the dramedy that is my life, the curtain's going down on this act. There will be a brief intermission, then the next act will commence." He opened the cover of the book in his hand and extracted a five-dollar bill. "And now I can visit the concession stand in the lobby."

I laughed and went back to work.

Author's note:

The faculty promotion process is an enormous deal to all faculty, whether at community colleges or universities. Having been through it three times myself, and having chaired our college's promotion committee, I can attest to the fact that it can be a hair-raising experience.

The promotion sequence that I describe in this book is, as best as I can tell from my research, how it's handled at Santa Monica College. I apologize for any errors. The process is entirely different at the community college where I work and, to my knowledge, our board of trustees has never interfered. I'm sure the real-life SMC board would never do so, either.

The board members that I've described are built from my own experiences. In my state, boards are appointed by the governor, so are not accountable to anyone else. Governors usually reward major campaign donors with positions on community college boards - whether the person knows anything about education or not. Currently, no one on our board has ever been in a classroom. In our state, that's business as usual.

In California, community college boards of trustees are elected officials, accountable to the citizenry. I'm jealous.

Thanks to my writing group: Becca, Bryan, Chris, Dustin, Jenn, Maggie, Michael and Michelle. Thanks to Stephanie at October Design Co. for the cover, thanks to Jon Michaelsen for the free publicity, and thanks to Josh Lanyon for allowing me to participate in her book launch party.

And, thanks to all my readers! I appreciate you more than I can say.

Connect with me...

At my blog: http://megperrybooks.wordpress.com/
On my Facebook page: http://facebook.com/jamiebrodiemysteries/
At Smashwords:
https://www.smashwords.com/profile/view/MegPerry2
At Amazon: http://goo.gl/D9VjhT

CPSIA information can be obtained
at www.ICGtesting.com
Printed in the USA
BVOW06s1920131117
500313BV00009B/439/P

9 781546 946069